Icthus

Stephen Olar

Bible Studies Available:

Other titles Available at Amazon.com
Bible Studies:
The Bible School Dropout's Bigger and Better Guide to Bible Study
The Bible School Dropout's Guide to More Bible
The Bible School Dropout's Guide to Building the Word of God in My Life
The Bible School Dropout's Guide to Hebrews
The Bible School Dropout's Guide to Dispensationalism
The Bible School Dropout's Book of Charts
The Bible School Dropout's Guide to Genesis 1-11
The Bible School Dropout's Guide to Genesis 12-26
In Hot Pursuit: Twelve Things God Wants Us to Pursue – Xtreme Xianity
Core Elements
The Name of the Lord is... Volume One: Pretty Awesome, Great, Glorious and Like Totally Excellent!
The Name of the Lord is... Volume Two Hi! I'm God
The Name of the Lord is... Volume 2.5 Hi! I'm Still God
The Name of the Lord is... Volume 3: The Great I AM
The Name of the Lord is... Volume 4: From Aleph to Tav- Print and E-books versions available
Everything I Needed to Know About Preaching, But No One Ever Told Me!
Novels:
Free – Print and E-book editions available
Icthus – Print and E-book editions available

Notices:

Icthus

Acknowledgments

I would like to thank Janis "Eagle Eyes" Ambel whose help was invaluable in working to revise the manuscript for this relaunch. I was much embarrassed to discover I had been blind to so many typos, grammatical errors and punctuation. She has her own book, you know: a wonderful biography of her late husband, who discovered and used his lifelong love of music to help overcome the horrors of World War II and brought Opera to a hockey-crazed steel town. You can find **Mr. Opera** on Amazon.com in both paperback and Kindle formats.

Where would I be as a writer if it wasn't for my beautiful wife of 30 years? She has put up with my obsession with words and the need I have to put them onto paper or cyberspace. Love you Brenda.

Icthus

Chapter One

Justin hunkered down in the predawn darkness. It wouldn't be too long now. His team was in place; the trap ready to be sprung.

There was a chill in the early spring air. The trees were just starting to bud. He remembered this place from his childhood and teen years. It was called The Bluffs. A hiking trail wound its way up the cliffs to the top where it commanded a glorious view of the valley below.

A portion of the cliffs were also home to a family of peregrine falcons, a project to reintroduce the almost extinct species back to its native habitat. The project was successful and the falcons were a common sight now along the cliffs.

Justin and his friends had often hiked up there and gathered around a campfire built to keep the night chill at bay. Occasionally, they would bring camping gear on warm summer nights. They would watch the stars and talk about the things of life teen age boys usually discuss, like girls, the upcoming football season, or girls hockey, or girls, soccer and girls.

Often in the fall season the church youth group would trek up The Bluffs to hold a wiener roast. Usually someone brought a guitar and they would pass the time away singing worship choruses that most of them knew from memory. As a teen, Justin would occasionally bring a girlfriend up here for a romantic picnic and alone time.

In the spring many people from the local church would hike up The Bluffs in time to see the sunrise on Easter morning to acknowledge the anniversary when Jesus rose from the dead.

To Justin that was a lifetime ago when he too believed such fairy tales. Now it was a world where everyone worked together to form a global community. On which had no place for ancient myths that propagated the idea there were any gods, let alone only one. He lived in a society were absolute truth was another fairy tale. He learned a long time ago that he was the master of his universe.

A sound that did not belong in the quiet woods snapped him out of his reverie and brought his attention back to the present. He looked out from his hiding place where he could see a good part of the hiking trail. He put on his night vision goggles.

About half way down the trail he could discern people shapes moving in the darkness. The person in the lead was dropping glow sticks on the path. Every 15 yards or so Justin could see a stick light up then drop to the ground. His lip curled up into a small smile. He spoke softly into his headset, "Team Leader to Team One. Targets are in sight."

"Copy that Team Lead. All are in position."

Justin watched as the leader cracked another glow stick and dropped it. It wouldn't be too much longer now. He licked his lips in anticipation. Soon he would snuff out another group of subversives.

Justin was familiar with dealing with such groups. It didn't matter if it was a bar fight, food riot or a Bible study. He treated them all the same. Illegal activities which needed to be stopped at all costs.

He shifted his position slightly to give him a better view from his vantage point. He saw the leader drop another glow stick. Justin glanced at his watch. Sunrise would be in about 30 minutes. He was anticipating a good haul this morning. After all it was the holiest days on the Christian calendar. They should be arriving in the clearing in the next 5 minutes or so.

"Check on position," he whispered into his mike.

His team verified their positions. They would not move until the signal was given. They knew that they would be taking no prisoners back with them today. These people had their chance to join society, but chose instead to embrace an ancient religion which had no place in the modern world.

Justin shook his head as he thought about his innocent childhood in this rural part of Northern Ontario. He and Caleb spent their summer days alternating fishing and swimming at the Grotto, tubing down the river or playing a pickup game of scrub in the back field behind their houses.

Then there was church. It started with Vacation Bible School, then going to Sunday school and the weekly Bible club. Caleb was right into that stuff and Justin would go along to support his friend. He had to admit most of the time he did have a good time.

When they got older and had to take that long bus ride to the city for high school, they were introduced to varsity football, then hockey and cross country in the spring. But then there was the summer. Even when they started to work and earn their own spending money, they were inseparable on their days off. During the first couple of years

Justin became more interested in the party scene on weekends. Caleb tried to understand why his friend was so interested in the booze and the loud music. He supported Justin and even attended a couple of parties with him. Finally Caleb told Justin that he could no longer go to those functions with him.

Justin sneered at the memory. "This stuff isn't honoring to God," Caleb would say. "I don't understand the reasoning for a person to get totally blitzed on alcohol and drugs and think they are having a good time."

Justin couldn't explain how the drinking and the dope helped him to escape what he felt was a dead end existence. He was biding his time when he could blow this pop stand and head for something bigger.

By the time high school had ended, the two friends went their separate ways. Justin went to University to study law and security, and then joined the armed forces and was recruited by Black Ops.

Caleb chose to spend a year at a Bible Institute before heading to university to study computer engineering. The two had touched base over the intervening years, but they never rekindled the brotherhood they had growing up.

The snapping of a twig brought Justin's attention back to the present.

Chapter Two

Justin watched his targets file into the clearing. Someone familiar with the location started a fire in the pit and they gathered around it to warm up while they waited for the rest of the group to arrive.

He could hear them talking quietly among themselves; sometimes a few would give a quiet chuckle during the course of the conversation. It seemed the stragglers had arrived for the talking ceased as the group formed a circle around the fire. A pale line of light marked the beginning of the sunrise.

As if a silent signal went out, the group started to sing. Justin listened to the song. Memories of Sunday morning filtered unbidden into his mind.

O Lord my God! When I in awesome wonder
Consider all the works Thy hands have made,
I see the stars, I hear the mighty thunder,
Thy power throughout the universe displayed.

He shook his head. It was hard to believe he still remembered the song, and was even starting to hum it in his head.

Then sings my soul, my Savior God to Thee;
How great Thou art! How great Thou art!
Then sings my soul, my Savior God to Thee;
How great Thou art! How great Thou art!

The group fell silent after at the end of the final chorus the sound of their voice echoing off into the distance, fading away. *How great Thou Art!* some people stood with their heads bowed, some with faces raised to the sky, hands held high. One of the men in the group began to pray. "Heavenly Father. We come here this morning to honor You and Your Son Jesus, whom You gave so many years ago to buy our salvation. We gather together this morning to remember the resurrection of our Lord and Savior."

He fell silent and another began to speak as well. "Thank you for coming out this morning." The voice had a familiar timber to it and Justin creased his brows. "You show your faithfulness to God this morning by taking the risk to openly worship Jesus Christ in a world that no longer tolerates Him or those who follow Him."

Justin could see people around the fire nod their heads in silent assent. He couldn't tell who was speaking but the voice was hauntingly familiar. It was still too dark to identify anybody at this point. He had to wait to spring the trap until he could clearly identify them for the record.

The voice continued. "We come together this morning, just as our brothers and sisters all over the world are doing to remember the resurrection of our Lord Jesus Christ. We no longer meet in buildings designated for that purpose, but we are still the Church and we are called to be a witness and a light in this dark place."

The disembodied voice stopped for a minute. The silence lasted for a few more, thenthe singing started again.

Low in the grave He lay, Jesus my Savior!
Waiting the coming day, Jesus my Lord!

Up from the grave He arose,
With a mighty triumph o'er His foes;
He arose a victor from the dark domain,
And He lives forever with His saints to reign,
He arose! He arose! Hallelujah! Christ arose!

Vainly they watch His bed, Jesus my Savior!
Vainly the seal the dead, Jesus my Lord!

Justin shook his head. He couldn't understand why people would still believe this drivel. The sun was fast arising. He spoke into his mike. "Get ready. We are set to roll on my mark."

He tensed, ready to spring into action. He had a baton in one hand and his pistol in the other. Justin could hear that person start to speak again. He recognized the words being spoken. *"For I received from the Lord that which I also delivered to you: that the Lord Jesus on the same night in which He was betrayed took bread; and when He had given thanks, He broke it and said, 'Take, eat this is My body which is broken for you; do this in remembrance of Me.'"*

They started to pass something from hand to hand. Justin recognized it as matzo bread. They were breaking off pieces of it and passing it from person to person. They were breaking bread. Justin was familiar with the practice although it had been many years since he had participated in the simple ceremony which recognizes the sacrifice Jesus had made.

He listened quietly as they started the next part of the ceremony. *"In the same manner He also took the cup after supper, saying, 'This cup is the new covenant in My blood. This do, as often as you drink it, in remembrance of Me.'" For as often as you eat this bread and drink this cup, you proclaim the Lord's death till He comes."*

Ok. Enough was enough. He spoke one word into his mike, "Mark."

His team exploded out of their hiding places. "You are under arrest for activities deemed subversive by the Government of Canada!"

People stood frozen for several seconds until a scream filled the air. The stasis broke and they moved to escape into the darkness. Instead they were caught in the snare of Justin's team. The squad performed to Justin's expectations and they started to club the targets or fire their Tasers at them. People were lying on the ground. All around were the cries of pain, and weeping. Victims were holding themselves or those who were now silent. The ground was beginning to take on the color of the blood that was seeping from the inflicted wounds.

Justin noticed one man was standing silently be the fire observing the mayhem around them. He was staring at him. Justin moved towards him with a sense of familiarity growing in his mind as he stared back at the shadowy figure. He approached the fire. Justin's face registered the shock as he recognized this person. Caleb!

Chapter Three

The two eight-year old boys squared off in the lane that led to the old farmhouse. Caleb's best buddy, Chris, had moved with his parents to Saskatchewan earlier that summer and Caleb missed him a great deal.

Now a couple of weeks before school began for the year a family had moved into the vacant farm house. Caleb stared across a big mud puddle, not sure what to make of the newcomer. He decided to race his new banana seat 3-speed through the muddy water when he noticed the strange boy standing on the other side. It was a bummer. Caleb was looking forward to the big splash the bike would have made. "Who are you?" He asked.

"Name's Justin. We just moved here from Sudbury."

Caleb moved closer to look at the new kid. He wasn't sure about him yet. Would he be a good tree climber? Being a townie, he probably didn't know how. "Do ya like ta fish?'

Justin, hands in his pocket, kicked at a dirt clod on the side of the driveway. "Sure."

"Can you climb trees?"

"I suppose."

Caleb, who had been straddling the bike dismounted and walked around the puddle. It was a waste of a good splash to ride through it from this short distance. He moved closer to Justin. "Do you have a bike?"

"Yeah. What's your name?"

"Caleb." He pointed to the house near the road, beside the lane. "We live in that house right over there. Have you been in the barn yet?"

Justin shook his head indicating he had not explored that building on the property yet. "Mom said not to go in there, it could be dangerous."

Caleb shook his head. "Nah. There's a rope in there and we can swing from it. Old Mr. Stewart put it there."

"Who is Mr. Stewart?"

Caleb pointed to the house Justin's family was in the process of moving into. "He's the old man who used to live here. Mom and Dad say he died feeding his pigs."

Justin's eyes grew big. "Wow! Do you suppose his ghost is still around walking in the barn?"

"Dunno. Maybe we could find out. Why don't you get your bike and we'll go for a ride."

Justin face brightened. "Sure!"

The two boys headed back toward the farmhouse. "How old are you?" asked Caleb.

"Eight. Birthday's in February."

"Cool!" responded Caleb. "Mine too. We'll be in the same class at school."

Justin shrugged. "I suppose. Are there a lot of kids around here?"

Caleb paused to think about the answer. He pointed towards the west. "There is Janie and Tessa. They live in the last two houses on this stretch."

He turned and pointed to the other direction. "Down that way Duncan, Cathy, George, Jo and Willie live."

"Duncan?" responded Justin. "Like the cake mix?"

Caleb giggled. "Nah. He said he was named after an old uncle in Scotland. Where ever that is. But there a lot of other kids who live on the other side of the highway. But mom won't let me ride my bike over there."

By that time they had reached Justin's house. Caleb set the kick stand and followed Justin into the house. "Hey, mom! This is Caleb. Can we go bike riding?"

Mrs. Jones pulled straightened up from the cupboard she was putting pots and pans away in and looked at the two boys. "Did you put your belongings away yet, young man?"

Justin nodded. "Well, Everything I found to put away. I'm soooo bored, Mom. Pleeeeze?"

Mrs. Jones looked as Justin and then at Caleb. "Well, Justin, why don't you introduce us?"

"Sorry, Mom. Caleb lives in the house at the end of our laneway. He has a bike and fishes."

She smiled. "So, Mr. Caleb. You ride a bike and fish? That would be pretty impressive for Justin here. He doesn't know how to fish yet. "

She looked back over to her son as he groaned in embarrassment. "Moooom!"

"Yeah. I suppose it's ok if you go out and play for a while. Be back in time for supper."

Just then there was a knock at the door. Mrs. Jones started down the hallway towards the sound. She saw a woman's face at the screen door. "Yes?"

The other woman smiled. "I'm Brenda White. I see you have already met my son, Caleb."

"Carol Jones." She motioned for the other woman to come in. She was cradling what looked like a potato salad with one arm. With the other she reached out to shake the first woman's hand. "A few of the neighborhood ladies will be stopping by today with some goodies for your supper tonight. We know how stressful moving into a new place can be."

Carol smiled and shook the proffered hand. "Why thank you. Do you have time for a cup of coffee?"

Brenda smiled and nodded.

Carol motioned her to follow her into the kitchen. The two boys fidgeted, looking for an opportunity to make there escape to the outdoors where there was a world to explore.

She took the heavy bowl and set it on the table, then motioned to the boys. "They were just getting ready to leave for a bike ride. Mine is Justin."

Brenda nodded. "It's a pretty safe area around here. There are a lot of young families and most of the kids go from house to house to hang out with their friends." She turned to them. "Well Justin, it is a pleasure to meet you. Son why don't you take Justin out and introduce him to the neighborhood?"

The boys didn't need to be told twice and bolted out the door. They heard their mothers laughing as the screen door slammed behind them.

Chapter Four

They rode through the puddle at full tilt, sending up waves of muddy water as they raced up the laneway towards the road. Caleb took the lead and turned right on the road heading for the gravel pit around the corner. It had some neat hills where they could jump their bikes over.

Caleb peddled furiously down one side of the pit and up the mogul hill. He sailed over the other side, letting out a whoop as he sailed through the air. Justin followed suit. He pulled up beside the other boy and they grinned at each other. "That is so neat!" declared Justin. "We lived in town and never had anything like this."

Caleb started peddling again and weaved in and out through a bike path the neighborhood kids had carved. Weaving through wash outs and gullies, they came out on a dirt road. Caleb looked back to see if Justin was still following. He saw he was and kept on.

Justin caught up with him on the road and they biked to the top of a steep hill. They stopped peddling and coasted down, the breeze whipping their hair. They reached the bottom of the hill, the momentum carrying them to the corner. Caleb stopped and Justin pulled up beside him. They were gazing down upon a body of water.

Justin though it looked like a river. It wasn't very wide. "This is a pond off the river," Caleb explained. "It's a good spot to catch smallmouth."

Justin wrinkled his brow. "What's a smallmouth?"

Caleb looked at his new friend with surprise. "You don't know what a smallmouth is?"

Justin shrugged. "Sure, I do. I was wondering if you did."

Caleb rolled his eyes. "It's a kind of fish, you dork. Come on."

They continued along the dirt road, climbing up a smaller hill. To the right was a tired old house, white paint peeling off the sides and more than a few shingles on the roof curling with age.

Caleb barely slowed as he turned into the driveway and stood as he pumped his legs harder on the pedals to get up the steep incline. Justin worked just as hard to keep up with the other boy.

They were breathing hard by the time they reached the house. Caleb stopped to catch his breath. He looked up and grinned at Justin, then hopped off the bike and let it drop to the ground.

He ran to the house into the lean-to porch on the side and knocked on the door. Justin stayed on his bike. The door opened and he could hear Caleb. "Hey, Mrs. C. Is Jo here?"

He couldn't see who Caleb was talking to but in a few seconds he was running back towards him with a girl in tow. A girl? Justin frowned. Girls were yuck! All they wanted to do was play with dolls and make believe house.

Caleb slid to a stop and looked at his new friend. "Hey, Justin, this is JoAnne. Jo for short."

Jo smiled at him. "She's the best tree climber ever!" exclaimed Caleb.

Justin had his doubts. Girls were not good at tree climbing: at least the ones he knew. But as he was the new kid, he had to accept Caleb's word on her ability. "Hi."

"Hi." said Jo. She pulled a battered baseball cap from the back pocket of her worn jeans and jammed it on her head backwards. "What're we doing today?"

Caleb shrugged. "Dunno. We were just riding around. Showed Justin the gravel pit."

"Did ya show him the fort yet?"

Justin's ears perked up. "A fort? Really?"

Jo had turned around and was heading back towards the house to get her bike. "Yeah, but it's a secret. If we take you there, you can't tell anyone."

Justin was impressed. This girl was more like a boy than a girl. If all girls liked biking and secret forts, he would be more inclined to like them too. Moving here away from all his friends in the city may not be so bad after all.

Icthus

Chapter Five

By the time school started Justin, Jo and Caleb had become fast friends. Jo and Caleb had introduced him to all the kids their age in the neighborhood. He caught his first small mouth bass, a small walleye and even a catfish.

They showed him the swimming hole at the river by the bailey bridge. Someone had tied a long rope from a tree overhanging it. The two showed him how to hold the rope, take a quick run and jump off the bank, swinging out over the water and drop into the cool river depths.

Just down from the rope swing was a bank made of clay. They made slides on the slippery surface, splashing into the shallow water along that part of the river and scrambling up the slope to do it again. When they got bored with that one they moved a little down the bank and created another one.

 The highlight of Justin's remaining summer was getting to see the fort. Jo and Cal biked down a small rutted path that ran from the barn to the back fields. "See that tall pine over there?" he called out to Justin.

Justin glanced in the direction Caleb had indicated. Standing above the other trees was a stately white pine. "Yeah."

"It's over there. You're gonna love it!"

When they got to the end of the fence line, they turned right and followed another trail. After a few minutes they stopped and jumped off their bikes. They walked along another trail through a wall of small pine and poplar trees. Pushing through them they were standing under the tree Caleb had pointed out.

Justin looked around. The kids had scrounged boards from their homes and had nailed them to the tree, forming a corner of sorts. Smaller boards also nailed to the tree created a ladder going up the broad trunk.

There were some old lawn chairs and a couple of small tables set up on one side under the branches. Caleb pointed up. "If you climb up there, you can see almost everyone's houses."

Their fort was generic enough that they could turn it into whatever they decided the game would be that day: a robber's hideout, a spaceship, a castle or even a pirate ship. Justin liked the freedom they had living in the country. In town his mother was so worried that he would be hit by a car or kidnapped by some stranger. He was only allowed to go to the local park or to a friend's house.

It was time for the start of a new school year. Caleb and Justin stood at the end of the driveway on that cool September morning waiting for the big yellow bus. They had seen it turn down the road where Jo lived. It was now on the return trip and they could see it approaching the main road.

They wiggled in their stiff new school clothes. They adjusted their backpacks to make them more comfortable on their shoulders: not that there was much in them, only their gym shoes and lunch pails. Their new teachers would give them a list of what they would need for their classes.

Justin begged to go on the bus with the rest of his friends. His mother was the new first grade teacher at Mountain View Public School. She had wanted to drive him there with her. In the end, with a little help from Caleb, she relented and allowed him to stand out at the end of the driveway with Caleb and the other kids.

Justin felt it was bad enough to have his mother teaching at the same school. He wanted to feel that he was the same as the other kids. He envied Caleb and Jo because their mothers stayed at home. When they got home from school, they would have snacks waiting for them. He would have to go home with his Mom. It was not cool to have a mother for a teacher.

Caleb was pointing out the names of the kids he had not introduced to Justin yet. By the time the bus reached the main highway and headed for the school, it was full of kids. Talking excitedly about their summers and some of them even looking forward to when they got to the school.

There were four other busses parked in front of the school when they arrived. Hundreds of children were milling about, being directed on where to go by teachers holding up big signs with numbers on them. It took Justin a minute to realize the numbers were the grades. Each teacher was holding up a sign with the grade he or she was in charge of.

They quickly located the teacher with the Grade Three sign. She was real pretty. She had long blond hair and smiling blue eyes. Her name was Miss McKenzie. The third grade boys had immediate crushes on her. Caleb nudged Justin in the ribs and whispered to him, "Don't worry, I won't tell anyone about -- you know – about your mom."

Justin gave him a grateful look and followed his new teacher into the building.

Icthus

Chapter Six

Justin's classmates eventually discovered his mother was the first grade teacher. The children razzed him a bit, but there were more important things in the world of a third grader than your mom being a school teacher. That was for little kids.

They were learning stuff like how to write cursive instead of print, collect autumn leaves for their science project and whose turn it was to look after the classroom pet; a black and white guinea pig named Toky.

The quarter quickly settled into its usual routine. There were the weekly pizza days, trips to the city library and a visit to the corn maze in October at a pioneer farm.

The boys raced each other through the maze, attempting to be the first out the other side. When they reached the exit, they would run back to the entrance to do it again. Caleb and Justin managed to navigate the maze three times before stopping for some hot chocolate and s'mores.

They pretended they were Batman and Robin for Halloween, yelling "Trick or Treat!" throughout the neighborhood until their pillowcases bulged with candy, chips and cans of pop.

After school, Justin would often end up at Caleb's house waiting for his mother to arrive home. If the weather was uncooperative they would watch TV and eat the chocolate chip cookies still warm from the oven. When the weather was still good they would go outside after their snack. Caleb's mother rarely had to shoe them out of the house to go and play, they had energy to burn from sitting all day in school.

Usually Jo would join them in their adventures. Either she would bike over to Caleb's or they would head over to her house. There were other friends that would join them in their after-school activities, but these three were usually found together most of the time.

One of their favorite spots to play was in the old barn on Jones' farm. It was two stories high. A ramp went up to the loft where hay and grain were stored. The lower part was reserved for the animals. Hanging from the main beam was a thick rope. They would take turns taking the rope and swinging across the bay giving a Tarzan-like yell and landing into piles of soft straw.

They would also take turns dropping down the hay shoot, landing where the hay was forked down and fed to the waiting animals. The lower part of the barn was mostly empty. Mrs. Jones was planning to get some chickens and pigs when they were fully unpacked and settled in.

If the weather was particularly nice, they would spend some time at the fort, often climbing up the tree to almost the top to see their world. But as the days turned from October to November and the snow began to fly, more time was spent indoors. The snow wasn't quite deep enough for outdoor activities yet.

School let out for Christmas and the kids, arms filled with the presents and goodies from their classroom parties, raced to the waiting busses to take them home for the break.

Caleb and the gang took Justin over to the gravel pit to go tubing. He asked his dad to get a couple of car tire inner tubes from Canadian Tire. Mr. White complied, even getting a couple extra ones for good measure.

They trudged to the top hill at the gravel pit. Jo and Duncan were already there. Jo had a Crazy Carpet and Duncan a toboggan. They took turns running along the top of the hill then throwing themselves on their conveyances, giggling and laughing as the wind whipped their faces and the snow flew up covering them in fine white powder.

It wasn't too long until the four of them were sitting on one of the inner tubes. They interlocked their arms and pushed themselves off. The tube picked up speed and hit a bump, causing the inner tube to bounce as it continued down the hill.

The kids finally fell off, rolling over each other from the momentum of the tube. They finally came to stop a big tangle of arms, legs, hats, coats and mitts gasping for air and laughing. They untangled themselves and raced after the inner tube, which free from its burden, continued to sail lightly over the snow.

Caleb jumped on it and dug his toes into the snow to stop the runaway tube. He was successful and they made their way to the top of the hill to do it again.

After an afternoon in the snow, they went back to one of their places where the designated mom would have some hot chocolate and other goodies ready for them. There were a lot of baked goods in the house this time of year, as people prepared for the hordes of relatives and friends that usually descend on each other's homes during the holiday season.

Christmas morning came and the Jones' and Smith's phones started ringing bright and early as Caleb and Justin called each other to report on the gifts they had just opened.

They were not all that excited when it came time to go back to school in a new year, although the parents' expressed their relief that the routine was back to normal.

Justin and Caleb celebrated their birthdays together. Their mothers combining their efforts. The house rang with laughter as third graders played pin the tail on the donkey and bag toss. The boys worked on grossing out the girls by opening their mouths and showing the half-chewed food.

Icthus

The kids went home filled with hot dogs, chips, pop, cake and ice cream and loot bags full of goodies and treats. The birthday boys thanked their guests for coming and for the gifts they received. Brenda and Carol breathed a sigh of relief it was over and retired to the kitchen to visit over a pot of tea.

Chapter Seven

School had been out for almost a month when Caleb burst into the fort waving a piece of paper around. Justin, Jo, and Duncan were there. They were already bored with summer. There was only so much swimming, fishing, biking, and hiking one could do before they were complaining about nothing to do. "Guess what I got?" he asked.

Duncan looked up from the Justice League comic he had been reading. "A piece of paper, you dork."

Justin threw a pine cone at him. "Gopher guts! Some teenagers are going door to door, handing these out. They called them invitations. You probably have one at your house too."

Justin jumped down from the low branch he was hanging from and walked over to Caleb. He grabbed the paper out of his friend's hand and looked at it. "You are invited to Vacation Bible School." he read. "What's Vacation Bible School?"

Caleb shrugged, "I don't know. I think the Bible has something to do about God. I'm not sure I like the school part. "

Justin continued to read the flyer. "It says there are games, horseback rides, crafts, Bible stories and a treasure hunt. This could be a lot of fun. I've never ridden a horse before."

He looked at the faces staring back at him. "Do you want to go?'

The kids looked at each other. Jo said, "I suppose so. We are going to have to ask our parents if we can go."

With the decision made they jumped on their bikes and peddled furiously to their respective homes to get parental permission.

It didn't take too long for them to gather again at the fort. "Mom said it was ok," reported Jo to the others.

The other kids quickly affirmed they had also received permission to attend the Vacation Bible School. Their mothers were also getting tired of their offspring claiming boredom from lack of activities, except when there were chores to do. Then the kids found something interesting to do.

The invitation said the week-long program started at nine a.m. on Monday. It was still only Thursday. The kids had never been to such a thing before and were excited to be checking out something new. Suddenly summer became more interesting again.

Chapter Eight

The boys were excited when Monday morning arrived. They were standing by the side of the road waiting for their ride at eight-thirty like the flyer said. Around the corner came a big blue bus.

Their excitement abated slightly at the sight of a bus coming down the road, regardless of the color. It brought back memories of school. But it stopped in front of them and the doors opened for them. A banner along the side said. "All Aboard for Vacation Bible School!"

The bus driver, an elderly gentleman in denim overall, plaid shirt and a ratty straw hat on his head smiled down at them. "Are you two coming to Vacation Bible School?"

Caleb spoke up first, "Yes, sir."

"Well, come on! We've got a busy morning!"

They clambered aboard and saw a lot of their friends already there. Jo excitedly waved at them from her seat and they made their way down the aisle to where she was.

A teenage boy Caleb had not seen before motioned for them to sit down. The doors closed and the bus started up again. The teen smiled at the children. "Ok kids, let's sing another song! How about *This Little Light of Mine*?"

He held up his hand and stuck up his index finger. "Everybody have your lights shining? Let's go."

Sounds of kids singing the song at the top of their voices rang out of the open windows as the bus sway along to its next stop. It wended its way along the road, stopping to pick up more children waiting to go to Vacation Bible School.

The bus was filled with laughing and singing children. The teen leading the singing was doing his best to make his voice heard above the cacophony.

The bus crossed the main highway and chugged up the hill on the other side. It turned into the driveway just over the crest. A stately oak tree guarded the entrance. Caleb noticed that a chain was sticking out of one side of it.

They pulled into what appeared to be the parking lot of a farm. The odor of manure filling the air. Caleb wrinkled his nose at the smell and then his eyes in puzzlement. He had never seen a parking lot at a farm before.

The bus pulled to a stop. The kids piled out and looked around. At one end of the parking lot was a big hole. Beside the hole was a beat up back hoe. Saw horses were set up around it with a length of rope strung between them. One of several hand-made signs attached to the rope told the children there was danger there and do not cross.

More cars and trucks were pulling into the yard and parking by the bus. Each disgorged a load of kids. Caleb recognized many of them from school. He was looking around when he heard a person let out a big whistle.

The Elderly gentleman was standing in the center of the parking lot. He was whistling through his teeth and motioning for everyone to gather into a big circle around him.

When all the children and several adults were gathered in the circle, the man began to speak. "Welcome all you youngin's! Welcome to Northwood's Bible Chapel and our very first Vacation Bible School!"

"We are going to start our day by prayin' and then singin' a song."

He took off his hat and asked the boys to take off their baseball caps. "Dear Lord. We thank you for this beautiful day that you have provided for us. We pray that our hearts are prepared for your message today and that some of these precious children will accept you as their Savior. Bless our time today, In Jesus name, Amen."

He looked up and walked around the inside of the circle looking at the children. "Ok. How many of you know the song *For God so Loved the World*?"

A few hands went up. "By the end of the week you will all know it, cuz we are singing it everyday we're here."

The man in the center started to wave one arm directing the crowd. "For God so loved the world, He gave His only Son. To die on Calvry's tree. From sin to set me free. Someday He's coming back. Oh glory that will be. Wonderful His love for me."

The chorus died away and the man motioned for everyone to be quiet so he could speak.

He turned around viewing the circle of children again. "Well, isn't this a nice group of youngins. Welcome. Now we are going to divide you into groups by what grade you were in last year."

He called out the teachers and helpers for the various age groups and they lined up to follow the leaders to their designated areas. Caleb and Justin found themselves in the group of grade Three to Five. They followed another man called Mr. James up the hill to the barn.

It seemed that their class was to be in the barn loft. This was getting better by the minute, Caleb thought. If only real school could be held in a barn; that would be so cool.

They sat through a Bible Story about someone named Jesus and some fishermen. They got to go and play red rover and then had some juice and cookies.

Icthus

They worked on their craft for the week: gluing burnt wooden matches to a cardboard cross. They line the matches up according to lines drawn on the piece of cardboard.

After that they were brought back to the barn where there were tables and chairs set up. Cups of pencils and pencil crayons were positioned down the center of tables. At each chair was a duo tang with paper in it.

Mr. James told the kids to fill out the work page for day one, which was the lesson they had this morning. The teen age helpers sat down with the kids and worked with them to finish the work page; looking up information in books on the table called Bibles.

With that task finished, they were given small squares of paper with a magnet glued on the back of them. "This is your memory verse that you will get points for if you can say it tomorrow," said Mr. James. "You can win a prize if you get the most points by the end of the week."

They trooped the kids down to the parking lot where they started that morning and stood in a circle again. The old bus driver stood in the center again and called out, "Did you have fun today?"

A chorus of kids yelled out. "Yes!"

"What's that? I can't hear you!"

"YES!"

"Are you all planning to come back tomorrow?"

They screamed out, "YES!"

They boarded the bus and headed carefully down the driveway, the driver keeping an eye open for other kids running to get to the line of cars which brought them.

The bus pulled up to Caleb's stop. He paused by the driver's seat. "What's your name, sir?"

"Everybody calls me Doc. What's yours?"

Caleb told him. "Well, Caleb. Are you planning to come back tomorrow?"

Caleb nodded in the affirmative. "See you tomorrow."

Caleb turned to step off the bus. Caleb and Justin ran to their homes, reminding each other to meet at the fort as soon as lunch was done. Caleb burst into the house. "Mom! That was so cool!"

Caleb attempted to talk between bites of the sandwich she prepared for him. He told her about the bus driver with the straw hat, the Bible story and the game they played. "And tomorrow we are going on a hay ride! It is so much fun. Can I go back?"

His mother nodded. "Sure. I don't see why not."

He shoveled in the last of his meal and washed it down with a glass of chocolate milk. He stood up and started for the door when his mother stopped him with, "And where do you think you're going, young man?"

He skidded to a stop and looked up at her. She pointed to the dishes he left on the table. "Put them in the sink. Is your room clean?"

He walked back to the table and picked up the dirty dishes and carried them to the sink. "Room's clean, mom."

Now if I go there and look is it really gonna be clean or did you push everything under the bed?"

"Sheesh, Mom! I only did that once. You grounded me for a week."

She ruffled his hair and gave him a kiss on the top of his forehead. "Ok. Off you go to play with your friends."

Not waiting to be told a second time, he raced out the door, jumped on his bike and headed for the fort.

The second day lived up to Caleb's expectations. The boys and Jo jostled each other on the hay wagon and tossed the straw about as it wound its way through the trees in the field behind the barn. The tractor pulled wagon was coming to a stop by the barn. "Hey, want to go fishing this afternoon?" asked Caleb.

Justin and Jo nodded their agreement as they jumped down from the now almost straw-bare wagon.

Chapter Nine

Justin set his bobber and cast his line over to the line of weeds along the bank. According to Caleb that is where the smallmouth liked to hide. "So what do you think of all this Vacation Bible School stuff?" he asked.

Caleb shrugged. "I like it. I think the stories are really neat."

Justin glanced out over the water, a slight breeze wrinkling the surface. "I don't know. The hay ride was fun today. Did you see Duncan when he got that face full of straw?"

Caleb chuckled. "Yeah. He did look kinda funny with all that straw all over him. Like the scarecrow in the Wizard of Oz."

They heard a bike slide to a stop on the gravel road and looked up to see Jo heading down the bank, fishing gear in hand. "How's the fishin' guys?"

"Just a couple of nibbles." Justin answered.

Jo carefully baited her hook and cast it out, landing near where Justin had his line sitting. She sat down beside them and wrapped her arms around her legs. "Are you guys going back to Vacation Bible School tomorrow?" she asked.

Caleb nodded, "Yup. Did ya memorize your verse yet?"

Jo shook her head. "Not yet. Mom said we might have to go to town. Grandma is sick and we are going to see her when Dad comes home."

Justin jiggled his line, hoping the movement would attract the attention of a fish. "Is it bad?"

Jo looked out over the water. "Yes. Mom and Dad don't say a lot. Mom sits in the easy chair in the living room and cries when she thinks we're not around."

"Maybe you can stay at our house tonight," suggested Caleb. "That way you can come with us."

They talked for the rest of the afternoon. Jo ended up not staying at the White's house that evening. Nor was she on the blue bus as it picked up the kids for day three of Vacation Bible School.

When Caleb returned home that afternoon, the house smelled of baking and cooking. On the table was a cooling rack piled with un-iced cupcakes and muffins.

Caleb thought he could smell his favorite lasagna dish coming from the oven. "He walked over to peer through the glass of oven door. "How come there are two lasagnas in the oven, Mom?"

"Hi, honey. Jo's grandma passed away last night. The extra lasagna is for them."

Caleb looked at his mother. "But she said she was going to visit her yesterday."

Mrs. White sat in a chair and called him over to her. She gave him a hug. "Jo wasn't told how sick her grandmother was. She will need you as a friend to help her. Jo is going to be very sad and cry a lot."

Caleb loved his mother, but there was only so much hugging a nine year old boy would tolerate. He squirmed out of her grasp and looked up at her. "Can I go tell Justin and Duncan?"

She smiled at him. "You can, but they probably already know."

He had his lunch and headed out the door toward the fort. The boys were already there. To his surprise Jo was there as well. Her eyes were red from crying, but she was trying hard to smile when she saw Caleb push through the pine shrubs.

"Momma said that Gramma went to Heaven and I can't go visit her anymore."

Caleb sat down beside her and awkwardly put his arm around her. "I'm sorry."

She leaned her head on his shoulder. Fresh tears started pouring down her face. "I want to see Gramma!"

Caleb thought. "They talked about going to Heaven today at Vacation Bible School. Maybe Mr. James can tell you how you can go there too."

She sat up. "You think so?"

"I don't know. But if you come back tomorrow, we can ask him."

She nodded. "Ok. I'll ask Mom if I can go tomorrow."

They sat around the fort for the rest of the afternoon. The boys didn't feel much like fishing or riding their bikes. Jo rocked quietly in the corner of the fort. It was almost supper time before they left to go home. The boys accompanied Jo home and waited until she entered the house. They turned around and quietly biked home.

Icthus

Chapter Ten

Caleb was glad to see Jo on the Blue bus the next morning. He walked down the aisle and slid in beside her. Although the teen leader was getting everyone to sing, they sat quietly. He reached out and held Jo's hand. She smiled at him and gave a sniff. Her eyes bright with unshed tears. "I'm glad you're here," he whispered.

This was Thursday, the second last day of Vacation Bible School. To Caleb it seemed there were even more kids on the bus than before. By the time they reached the farm it was standing room only. The older children standing and letting the younger ones sit.

They stood in the circle, sang the opening song, prayed and then went to their classes. Mr. James talked again about Jesus. Caleb now understood this person was the Son of God and that He came to Earth to save people from their sins. He wasn't quite sure what that meant, but he was sure Mr. James could explain it.

They waited until the Bible lesson was done and the class filed out for their recreation period. They sat quietly in their chairs watching Mr. James as he busied himself putting his material away.

He turned around and saw Caleb and Jo sitting quietly. "Well, bless my soul." He said. "What is so important that you are missing the hike today?"

Jo looked at Caleb and leaned over to him. She whispered in his ear, "Can you tell him?"

Caleb nodded and looked back up at their teacher. "Sir, Jo's Gramma went to heaven yesterday and Jo wants to go and visit her."

Mr. James nodded. He didn't smile or chuckle at the request. He rubbed his chin with his hand. "I see. I am very sorry about your grandmother, Jo. We have been learning this week how we can get to go to Heaven."

He picked up his Bible and walked over to the two children. He turned a chair around and sat down, facing them. "It is a very hard thing when we lose someone we love." He touched his chest over his heart. "It hurts here and there feels like there is a big hole."

Jo nodded. She knew what he was saying. Caleb nodded too, but he wasn't sure what Mr. James was talking about. He realized that although Mr. James was talking mainly to Jo, he would glance over to him, including him in the conversation.

He paused, took a breath and continued. "That's how God felt when He sent Jesus to Earth. There was a big hurt in His heart. We had no chance of pleasing Him on our own."

"We all want to go to Heaven, but because of our sin, God would not allow it. All of us think that be being very good, or going to church every Sunday will please God enough to allow us to go to Heaven. But nothing we do will ever make us that good."

Mr. James opened his Bible and flipped through the pages. "One of our memory verses this week tells us how much God loves us. John 3:16; '*For God so loved the world that He gave His only begotten Son, that whoever believes in Him should not perish but have everlasting life.*'"

Jo nodded. That was the verse they were given on their first day. God knew that there was nobody who was good enough to get to heaven." He handed her his Bible, "Please read this verse; Romans 1:10.

'As it is written: "There is none righteous, no, not one;'

He looked at Caleb and Jo. "Do you know what the word righteous means?"

They shook their heads, "Well it means to be right. The verse is telling us there is no one right in God's eyes. It doesn't matter how good we are, we are not good enough for Him on our own. Jo, will you read verse 23, please."

Jo moved her fingers to the spot Mr. James indicated. "*For all have sinned and fall short of the glory of God.*"

"Do you know what it means to sin?"

Caleb looked at Mr. James. "It means that we've done wrong."

"That's very good, Caleb. That word means to 'miss the mark.' That's why the rest of the verse says we have fallen short of the glory of God."

"But that is where God steps in." He took the Bible from Jo and handed it to Caleb. "Please turn to Romans 5:10 and read it for us, Caleb.
He thumbed over a couple of pages and located the verse. "*But God demonstrates His own love toward us, in that while we were still sinners, Christ died for us.*"

He looked back up at Mr. James. "Remember in John 3:16 we read that God gave His only begotten Son?"

The children nodded. "Well that is what it was talking about, "The only one good enough to pay for our sins was Jesus Christ. He was God's answer to our problem. We have to die because of our sins, but God gave us a wonderful gift. Why don't you look up Romans 6:23 for us and read it."

"For the wages of sin is death, but the gift of God is eternal life in Christ Jesus our Lord."

Jo was fidgeting in her chair. "So how do I get to Heaven to visit my Grandma?"

Mr. James looked at her and smiled. "Jo, the only way to get to Heaven is by believing that Jesus Christ came to Earth to save you."

"I didn't know your grandmother, but she is there if she believed that. Do you understand?"

Jo and Caleb nodded. Mr. James continued. "The Bible says, *'For with the heart one believes unto righteousness, and with the mouth confession is made unto salvation.'* and *'For whoever calls on the name of the LORD shall be saved."*

Mr. James looked from Caleb to Jo. "If you want, we can pray right now and you can know that you are going to Heaven. Do you want to pray with me?"

Jo and Caleb looked at each other. They weren't sure what to say. After a few minutes, Mr. James spoke again. "If you want to think about it, we can talk anytime."

Jo shook her head. "I'm ready now. Will you help me?"

Mr. James smiled and nodded. "Ok. Let's talk to God and tell Him about your decision. Do you want to talk to Him or do you want to repeat after me?"

"I'll repeat after you."

The man slid forward and kneeled on the floor. Jo and Caleb did the same thing. "Dear God: I know I am not good enough to get to Heaven on my own. I am a sinner and your Word tells me that. But I believe you sent Jesus to save me from my sins. I ask for forgiveness and ask Jesus to come into my heart. Amen"

Jo repeated the prayer. There were tears in her eyes as she looked up at the teacher. "Thank-you. Now I will get to see Jesus and Gramma!"

Caleb was thoughtfully silent. Mr. James looked at him, his face showing an invitation to do the same. Caleb wasn't sure about it all. He wanted to think about the discussion they just had. "I want to think about it." He said at last.

Mr. James nodded, "fair enough. Thank you for listening to me today."

They stood up and Mr. James enfolded both of them in his arms. "You are very precious to God. Don't ever forget that."

He released them and looked at his watch. "Well we had better hurry. It is almost time for you to do your work page for today. I'm sorry you missed your recreation time."

"It's ok," said Caleb. "This is kind of important."

By now they could hear the excited talking of the other children as they raced up the ramp into the barn. They rushed for the tables and found their spots. Jo, now smiling, and Caleb went to join them.

Icthus

Chapter Eleven

Friday was the last day of Vacation Bible School. The highlight of the day was the treasure hunt. Jo, Caleb and Justin raced from clue to clue to figure out where the treasure was. Their team located it first, which was appropriately buried under a pile of dirt.

Caleb came in second in the week's contest and came home with a new Bible. His mother looked at it politely and smiled at his retelling of the morning's events. She was a little preoccupied as that evening was the wake for Jo's grandmother and Mrs. White was making egg salad and salmon sandwiches for it as well as the luncheon after the funeral tomorrow.

He had a couple of sandwiches, a glass of milk and headed out the door to go to the fort where they would discuss the day's events.

Caleb was the first to arrive. He opened his back pack and pulled out the workbook chronicling the week's activities.

Some of the verses Mr. James had them read yesterday were there, as well as the ones they had to memorize every day. He looked at the crossword puzzles and other activities he completed and reviews of the stories he heard.

Caleb put the book down and stared up. He could see clouds floating high above through the maze of pine branches.

He was puzzled with the conversation he and Jo had with Mr. James. A lot of what he said made sense. But Caleb wasn't sure. Jo was sure and had a big smile on her face this morning. "I feel so good," she said when he sat beside her on the bus. "I'm still sad about Gramma, but I feel better because I will see her someday."

They attempted to explain the events to Justin and Duncan yesterday at the fort, but with little success. They had gone with the rest of the class on their hike and were more interested in sharing about the stuff they encountered on their walk through the woods on the farm.

The last page of the workbook was an invitation to come to Sunday school at ten o'clock on Sunday morning. There would be singing and games and a Bible story, almost like Vacation Bible School.

Caleb thought about this. Most of the cool cartoons were on Saturday mornings. There were a couple he liked to watch on Sunday as well. He thought about missing them to check out Sunday school when Justin and Duncan pushed their way through the pine shrubs.

"Hey, Justin and Dun. Watch ya want to do today?"

Duncan watched as Caleb put the workbook back into his backpack. "How about fishing?" he suggested.

Caleb and Justin looked at each other and shrugged, "Why not?" Asked Justin. "Do you want to wait for Jo or will she meet us at the fishing hole?"

They decided not to wait for Jo. With her grandmother's passing, they weren't expecting her to show up. It was a pleasant surprise to see her bike on the side of the road. She wasn't fishing, but was sitting on the bank with her arms wrapped around her legs.

She didn't get up when she saw them coming. "Hey guys. Thought you might show up here today."

They looked at each other and nodded to her. Caleb slid down the bank and sat beside her. "We were wondering if you would even come out to play today, with your Grandma and all."

Jo's lips trembled as she gave a small smile. "I miss her so much. But I know that I'll see her someday."

The boys looked at each other. They weren't sure what to say about that. Jo continued, "I have Jesus in my heart. Caleb you were there when I did that."

Caleb nodded. He certainly had been there with her and Mr. James. But he wasn't sure what had happened. Jo still seemed sad, but she was no longer upset over her grandmother's dying. Mom said that sometimes people want to deny what they have experienced. It was the mind's way of coping with big things. "So are you going to go to the funeral tomorrow?" he asked.

Jo looked out over the water and back to the boys. "Mom said I could if I wanted to. It would be nice if you could come too."

This surprised the boys. They were not expecting this invitation to go look at a dead person. Caleb realized it was more than that, but he kept that to himself. Justin spoke up. "Um... We will have to probably ask our parents."

Jo smiled. "That's ok. There is something called a wake tonight. There is a special church service tomorrow morning. Does anyone know why they call it a wake? We are already awake."

Caleb had to giggle. It certainly didn't seem to make any sense. He would have to ask Mom when he got home.

As it turned out, Caleb did not have to ask his mother. Jo's mother had called her and asked if it was all right If Caleb came to the funeral home this evening to keep Jo company for the evening. Mr. White agreed immediately. She felt it was important not to shield a child from some of the harsh realities of life; including death.

She sat in her easy chair and motioned Caleb to come over to him. He cuddled up with her and she rocked him as she did when he was a baby. She stroked his hair. It wouldn't be much longer when he would not permit her to fuss over him like this. She enjoyed every moment.

"Caleb, I know we have already talked about Jo's grandmother and how Jo may show what she is feeling. But the next couple of days are going to be hard for her and her family."

"Tonight we are going to a place called a funeral home. It is a special building where people's bodies are prepared for burial.

We will be attending a wake. It is where we pay our respects to the family. That means we tell them how sorry we are for their loss and show that we support them while they are saying good-bye to their loved one."

"Jo's mother asked me if you would like to keep Jo company. I think that is a wonderful idea. But I don't want you to think it is a free for all.

Caleb looked up at her. "You will also see something that may be disturbing. You will see the physical remains of Jo's grandmother. They will have her made up to look like she's sleeping. She will be lying in a box called a coffin. Do you have any questions?

"Mom, Jo said she asked Jesus into her heart yesterday. Do you know what that means?"

His mother was silent for a few minutes. "I'm not sure what that means. When did this happen?"

"Jo was saying how she wanted to go to Heaven to see her grandma. The people at Vacation Bible School were talking about going to Heaven so we asked about it. Mr. James explained that one had to be saved to go to Heaven."

"He said you had to believe in Jesus."

Mrs. White nodded silently. "Well religious beliefs can be very important. But they are very personal."

"Mom, would you be angry with me if I said I wanted to go to Heaven too?"
She laughed. "Of course not, son. If you want to start attending church, I will not stop you from doing that."

He snuggled closer to her. "Would you come with me?"

She smiled. "I might son."

He cuddled with her for a few more minutes before he decided he had enough for today.

Icthus

Chapter Twelve

Caleb entered the funeral home walking beside his parents. The walls were dark wood and there were picture of people on the wall. Caleb read the plaques under some of these portraits and learned these were the funeral directors. He heard of band directors and movie directors, but this was new.

He was carrying a tray of sandwiches his mother had given him and she nodded with her head to go down the hallway where a sign stood stating the visitors' lounge was downstairs.

He followed his parents down to the lounge where he saw a long table filled with trays of sandwiches, cookies, squares as well as fruit, cheese and meat. He could smell coffee as well. "You can put your trays down on the table." Mrs. White said to her husband and son.

She turned and nodded to an elderly lady Caleb recognized from the chapel and they went back upstairs. Across the hall was a set of double doors. He could see people standing or sitting on living room chairs. They were all talking quietly to each other.

The Whites walked through the doors and Caleb could see Jo and her parents standing beside a long shiny dark brown box with the lid open on one end. The other end of the box was covered with flowers. To one side a line of people were waiting to speak to the family. Caleb's father stopped by a podium and signed the book laying open on it. They walked over to the end of the line and joined it.

Jo noticed Caleb and waved to him. He waved back and gave her a smile. Then he noticed she was wearing a dress. He could feel his eyebrows grow wide. This is the first time he had seen her in a dress. She didn't even wear them to Sunday school.

The line slowly moved closer to the casket. Caleb started to fidget. This was really boring. He could see lots of flowers behind the Collins and on the other side of the coffin.

They finally reached the front of the line. Caleb shook hands with Mr. Collins. Mrs. Collins gave him a hug. "Thank you for coming Caleb," she said softly to him.

He stood in front of Jo, feeling suddenly shy. She smiled at him. "I'm glad you're here!" She grabbed his hand and pulled him over to the casket.

The only experience Caleb had with dead bodies are those he saw on television, and most of the time, they were vampires or zombies. Jo's grandmother looked like she was sleeping peacefully. At any moment she would sit up and go make herself a cup of tea.

"Mom said I don't have to stay once you got here. I'm hungry."

Caleb looked over to his parents who were still chatting with the Collins. He caught their attention and asked if it was ok if he went with Jo. They nodded and the two went off in search of the food.

They noticed Justin and Mrs. Jones standing in line about ten people from the front. They waved at Justin, who after tugging on his mother's hand to get her attention, was allowed to join them.

They went down to the lounge. There were a few people sitting at the round tables, sipping from cups and chatting. The children went over to a long table laden with food and looked it over. Caleb had never seen so much at one time.

The elderly lady Caleb saw earlier spotted them and came over. She gave Jo a hug. "Hi, Sweetie. How are you doing?"

Jo returned the hug. "I'm ok Mrs. Smith."

She looked over at the two boys. "It is a really nice thing for you two to be here and show your support." She motioned to the table. "I bet you would like to try all of these goodies. I know I would!"

Mrs. Smith handed them small paper plates and napkins. She gave Jo another quick hug and walked back to the coffee makers to remove a fresh brewed pot.

The three filled their small plates with some cookies, brownies and some cheese and carefully carried them over to an empty table in the corner and sat down.

They nibbled on the treats and drank some juice Mrs. Smith brought over to them. They looked at each other, not sure what to say or do in this quiet environment. Jo downed her juice. "This is nice. I was getting so thirsty standing up there all that time. And my face hurt from smiling at so many people." She made a face. "All of them wanted to hug me and kiss me on the cheek."

Justin looked over to her and handed her a napkin. "Well that explains all the lipstick on your face."

Jo grabbed the napkin and quickly wiped her face. Caleb swallowed the brownie he had been chewing on." I thought this was going to be something really sad."

Jo nodded. "Yeah. Me too. But people are really nice. I still feel sad inside, but it is hard to cry when there are so many people."

More people were coming into the lounge and the kids decided to go back upstairs. There seemed to be even more people in the room than there was before. Caleb could see that Mrs. Collins was sitting in one of the living room chairs sipping a glass of water.

Jo took them back up to the casket so Justin could look at her grandmother. Caleb, not really wanting to look at her again went anyway because he didn't see any other kids.

After Justin has seen the body, Jo went back over to her mom and gave her a hug. Mrs. White came over and spoke softly with Mrs. Collins. She nodded and whispered to Jo then nodded to other the women.

Caleb's mother came over to them. "Come on kids, I'm going to take you for some ice cream. Would you like that? Justin, you can come too."

They were enthusiastic in their response and quickly followed Mrs. White out of the building.

Chapter Thirteen

The funeral was an entirely different mood.

Caleb looked around as he sat in the chapel of the funeral home. Its walls were painted a soft white. He could hear music coming from speakers in the ceiling.

People were not talking and visiting like they were last night. They were sitting quietly in the pews. A movement caught his eyes and turned his head. Doc was coming up the middle aisle carrying his Bible. He wasn't dressed in his denim coveralls today, but wore a suit.

He stepped up three stairs at the front of the room and stood behind the pulpit. Doc looked around and motioned for the gathering to stand. The music grew louder as people stood up.

Caleb was next to the aisle and could see the funeral director was pulling the coffin that held Jo's grandmother's body. The lid was now closed and the flowers that sat on one end last night sat on the middle of the box.

Jo's family followed the coffin. They were not smiling this morning. Jo was crying as she walked with her parents. Mrs. Collins' eyes were also red from crying.

Six men whom Caleb did not know walked behind them. They filed into the pews at the front of the chapel and stood with the rest of the people until the funeral director positioned the coffin at the front of the room

Doc motioned for the congregation to sit down. He opened his Bible. "Let us pray".

There was a soft rustle as people bowed their heads. "Father we come together to remember the life of Mrs. Pots. We grieve with her family because she will be sorely missed. We ask Your blessing on our service today. In Jesus name, Amen."

He looked up and smiled out at the people. "On behalf of the Collins' and Pots' families, I would like to extend a welcome and a thank you for the support you have shown them."

"I've only met this family recently. First with Joanne this week when she came to our little church for the first time this last week. Even at a young age, we are sometimes asked to bear heavy burdens. Through Jo I was privileged to meet her parents and Mrs. Pots other children and their families."

After the graveside service this morning, the family would like to extend an invitation to return here for a luncheon."

Doc rearranged his glasses and straightened his notes. He looked at the grieving family and then cleared his throat.

"Death is never easy when it comes, although it is an inevitable part of life. In the Book of Ecclesiastes we read *"To everything there is a season, and a time for every purpose under heaven;*

A time to be born, and a time to die; a time to plant and a time to pluck up that which is planted;

A time to kill , and a time to heal; a time to break down, and a time to build up;

A time to weep, and a time to laugh; a time to mourn and a time to dance;

A time to cast away stones, and a time to gather stones together; a time to embrace and a time to refrain from embracing;

A time to get, and a time to lose; a time to keep, and a time to cast;

A time to rend, and a time to sew; a time to keep silent and a time to speak;

A time to love, and a time to hate; a time of war, and a time of peace.

"Before I give the message this morning, some of the family members have some thoughts they would like to share with of their mother's lives. If anyone else would like to share, please do so."

He motioned for Mrs. Collins to come up to the pulpit and then stepped down from the pulpit and sat in the front row. Several other people followed, telling stories of Gladys life and what she meant to them. Caleb fidgeted in his seat. This part wasn't as interesting as last night.

Finally Doc came up and talked again about God and believing in Jesus and then closed the service with prayer. Music started up again and the funeral director motioned for the people to stand. He opened a side door Caleb had not noticed before and then directed the men in the front to come along side of the coffin.

They carried it out of the door. The family followed. Jo wasn't the only one crying now as they filed out behind the earthly remains of Gladys Pots.

Icthus

Chapter Fourteen

The funeral had been a turning point for Caleb. He thought more about death and what would happen to him if he were to die. Was he good enough to go to Heaven to be with Jo and her grandma? If Mr. James was right, then he wasn't.

His mom seemed to think that being a good person was ok. His dad didn't believe there was a Heaven and church was a waste of time. But he did not prevent Caleb from climbing aboard the blue bus Sunday morning when it drove by.

He accompanied Jo to Sunday school often. Justin would occasionally join them. But he did not seem all that interested in learning Bible studies.

They still met in the barn throughout the summer and early fall after the kids had returned to school. When the weather got too cold, they started holding Sunday school at someone's house.

It was spring time when they returned to the farm. But instead of going to the barn for their Sunday school class there was a new building at the end of the parking lot. Doc called it the chapel. His new classroom was in the back of the basement of the new L-shaped building: the last door on the right.

Mr. James continued on as his teacher, telling stories from the Bible and sending homework pages, memory verses and a paper with more stories in it that Caleb could read at home. Sometimes instead of going to Sunday school, he would hang out with Justin. Now that it was spring, it was time to break out the bikes and fishing gear again and get them ready for the upcoming summer.

They were in the Garage at Justin's place. Oiling can and rags in hand, they flipped their bikes upside down and turned the pedals with their hands, drizzling oil on the chain as it spun around the sprockets.

They used their tire gauges to check the air pressure and wiped down the frames. It was time to bring them out of their hibernation. The boys made it a point to speed through every puddle they could find. Laughing and peddling they headed to the gravel pit to see if the jumps they created last year survived the winter. Their shouts of delight confirmed that they were still there and raced toward them.

After Caleb and Justin re-conquered the moguls they headed back to Justin's for lunch. Mrs. Jones haade chicken noodle soup and grilled cheese sandwiches for them. They slurped the noodles, egging each other on as to who could make the biggest slurp sound.

Instead of going to the fort after lunch, they went to visit Jo. She would be home from Sunday school now and ready for play. She was almost back to her old self like she was before her grandma died.

What puzzled Justin was Jo's interest in going to church now. He sometimes didn't want to be around her because she would talk a lot about Jesus as if He were a real person. Occasionally he would go with her and Caleb to Sunday school but he was not all that interested in going on a regular basis.

Now Caleb went quite a bit, but he was still a pretty cool bud. Church didn't seem to change him the way it had changed Jo.

They spent the afternoon at Jo's place, watching TV and reading comic books. Caleb liked hanging out with Jo. She was a lot of fun to be with than most girls. She liked to climb trees, fish and ride bikes with them. She was one of the guys.

"You guys should have come to Sunday school today, you missed a neat lesson," she said as she turned the page of a new Archie comic.

Caleb tried to look uninterested. "Why?"

Justin yawned and continued to read Superman.

"They were talking about a man named Noah. God told him to build a big boat to save the animals because there was going to be a flood and He was going to drown everyone."

"Wow!" said Caleb, "That sounds so cool."

Jo nodded. "Yeah. It rained for forty days and nights. Mr. James said they were in the ark for over a year before the water went down enough so they could get out."

"Wow." said Justin. "And Mr. James didn't talk about Jesus?"

Jo sniffed at him and continued. "Of course he did. He said that this is a picture of how God protects us from being judged. Being in Jesus keeps me safe just like Noah being in the ark kept him safe."

"Not only that, they are already planning for Vacation Bible School this summer. They said it will be even better than last year's."

Caleb didn't think it was possible. "Oh?"

Jo nodded. "They said they are going to do the Wordless Book."

Justin wrinkled his eyebrows. "What kind of a book is that? No words?"

Jo shrugged. "Dunno. You'll just have to come to find out."

Caleb almost wished he had gone to Sunday school today. But Vacation Bible School was in July. And that was a long way from this fine Sunday afternoon in May.

Icthus

Chapter Fifteen

Caleb had to admit this year's Vacation Bible School had been the best one yet; even though he only had last year's to compare it to.

They didn't meet in the barn this year, but used the auditorium of the new chapel. Caleb would have preferred the barn, it was more fun there. Mr. James wasn't the teacher but a young woman named Miss Jane.

They still had horseback and hay rides and the big treasure hunt on Friday. They even had a wiener roast on the last day for the children and their parents.

He liked the Wordless Book. Even Justin was intrigued enough to come and find out how they made a book that didn't have any words.

Caleb placed his treasures from the week on his dresser and flopped down on his bed.

Caleb looked at his copy which he created along with the workbook from the week's lessons. He looked at the birdhouse which now graced the top of his dresser. It was the project craft for the week. Every day they worked on it, from sanding the pieces to painting it. His was a bright orange and yellow. Caleb was sure his dad would help him put it up outside.

He picked up the bracelet they also made. It was made of the same colors as the pages of the book.

He opened the book and looked at the first page. It was yellow and was about Heaven where God lived - and Jo's Grandma.

The next page was black. It represented his heart which was full of sin. Everyone's heart was like that; unable to go to Heaven because of the sin in their lives. This was not new to Caleb. He had heard Mr. James say the same thing last year when he talked with Jo.

He looked at the red page next. It represented the blood Jesus shed on the cross for his sins. Caleb still thought a lot about this. His mother said all people are good. He was not sure of that anymore.

The white page represented the person who believed that Jesus died for their sins. They were now considered right with God and allowed to go to Heaven.

The final page, green, was to remind him that it was important that when a person became a child of God, they should learn to love Him more and serve Him.

He went to Sunday school for the rest of the summer. In the fall Miss Jane became his new Sunday school teacher. Mr. James, he was told, was going to work with the young people. Caleb understood this meant the teenagers.

It was late September. In the Sunday school class Miss Jane was getting ready to teach the lesson for the day.

The children looked at each other as they approached their classroom. On the door was a black piece of Bristol board with fiery red lettering: Welcome to Hell.

Miss Jane opened the door and motioned them to go inside. She had covered the windows so it was really dark in the room. Instead of the normal fluorescent lighting, she had lamps with red bulbs in them. On the walls she had draped some red material. It was also very warm in the room. Caleb noticed a couple of portable heaters were glowing red.

Normally they would be talking with each other while she shushed them and would start her lesson for the day. Today they sat silently looking up at her.

"You know boys and girls, we talk a lot about going to Heaven and how much God loves us, but we never talk about what happens to those people who don't believe that Jesus is God's son and that He died for our sins. Today we are going to talk about that.

She picked up her Bible and opened it to the spot where she had placed a bookmark.

"Jesus was teaching the people one day when He told this story."

"There was a certain rich man who was clothed in purple and fine linen and fared sumptuously every day. But there was a certain beggar named Lazarus, full of sores, who was laid at his gate, desiring to be fed with the crumbs which fell from the rich man's table. Moreover the dogs came and licked his sores. So it was that the beggar died, and was carried by the angels to Abraham's bosom. The rich man also died and was buried. And being in torments in Hades, he lifted up his eyes and saw Abraham afar off and Lazarus in his bosom.

"Then he cried and said, 'Father Abraham, have mercy on me, and send Lazarus that he may dip the tip of his finger in water and cool my tongue; for I am tormented in this flame.' But Abraham said, 'Son, remember that in your lifetime you received your good things, and likewise Lazarus evil things; but now he is comforted and you are tormented. And besides all this, between us and you there is a great gulf fixed, so that those who want to pass from here to you cannot, nor can those from there pass to us."

She sat on the corner of the desk and looked at the group of children staring up at her. "The Bible uses the word "Hades" instead of "hell." This story gives us an idea of what this place was about. What did you learn from this story?"

Jo put her hand up. "It is a hot place."

Miss Jane nodded. "That's correct, Jo. Can someone else tell me something about this place?"

Caleb squirmed in his chair. It was warm and he could use a drink of juice. "The man wanted a drink of water, but couldn't have one."

"Yes, Caleb. We get that idea from what we read here. It tells us that the man was in torment and could not get relief from it."

"It is a place where Jesus is not. To be in Hell is to be separated from Jesus forever."

She turned some pages in her Bible. "We read in Psalm 9:17 *"The wicked shall be turned into hell, and all the nations that forget God.*

"A lot of you kids come to Sunday school most of the time, a couple all the time and a few hardly ever."

Caleb squirmed in his seat. He wished Justin were here today to listen to this. Miss Jane continued. "Hell is an awful place. It is a place of fire and darkness and pain."

She picked up a tray that had some powder on it and flicked a lighter. "This is Sulphur."

She touched the flame to the sulfur and immediately a rotten egg smell filled the room. Some of the kids started to choke and cough. Caleb, his eye watering, started to cough as well. Miss Jane put down the dish with the sulfur and opened the windows. The kids breathed the fresh air and sighed. They started to giggle.

Miss Jane smiled. "Yes, we can breathe fresh air and clear our lungs. But the people that go to Hell will not be able to open windows. They can't go to the fridge and get a pop. They can't even get a drop of water to cool their tongues."

"Why are they there? Because they did not believe the Jesus is the Son of God. All of us know John 3:16 right?"

All of the kids nodded. "But let's read the next couple of verses: *'For God did not send His Son into the world to condemn the world, but that the world through Him might be saved. He who believes in Him is not condemned; but he who does not believe is condemned already, because he has not believed in the name of the only begotten Son of God.'*"

"You see kids, if you want to go to Hell, you don't have to do anything at all. You are already on your way. If you want to go to Heaven, you have to believe that Jesus died for your sins and rose again."

Caleb knew that he didn't want to go to Hell. He knew enough to realize he wasn't good enough to get there. He already knew the words to say. He remembered them from the day Jo spoke them with Mr. James. He bowed his head and silently prayed.

"Dear Jesus, I want to go to Heaven to be with You. I'm not good enough to be there. The Bible says if I believe I will go to Heaven."

He opened his eyes and looked up. He was still in the classroom but he felt different. He was no longer afraid. He was going to Heaven!

"Miss Jane?"

"Yes, Caleb."

"I just gave my heart to Jesus. I am going to Heaven!"

Jo squealed and clapped her hands.

Miss Jane came over to him and knelt down in front and gave him a big hug. "Congratulations Caleb! Welcome to the family of God."

Icthus

Chapter Sixteen

Caleb, Justin, and Jo were floating down the river on the inner tubes they used the previous winter for racing down the frozen hills of the gravel pit. This was a big year for them. They were thirteen and headed for high school.

But it was August and school was three weeks away. Today they were enjoying themselves. With their parent's permission, they took the tubes and dropped them in the Grotto, a small tree covered island located in the middle of the river located just up the road from Jo's house.

They floated down the slow-moving meandering river to where it bordered on the back of the Jones' property. By road they were only a couple of kilometers apart: the river journey was closer to five.

Their mothers made them put on waterproof sunscreen as the effects of the sun on the skin would be magnified by the water.

Caleb leaned back, his feet and bum in the water. He gazed up at the blue sky, a few fluffy white clouds drifting by. The pine and birch trees were standing guard on the banks as they floated by them. A couple of dragon flies flitted along the top of the water. Justin broke the silence. "So what do you think about traveling 45 minutes to school every day instead of 10?"

"Well, it means we have to get up earlier than now," commented Caleb. "But it should be cool for you; your mom won't be there to protect you."

"Bite me, White!"

Jo laughed. "I'm looking forward to it. We have officially outgrown elementary school and are ready to move on."

Justin snorted. "At least there will be lots of girls."

Caleb nodded. "Yeah!"

Jo shook her head. "Ah, you two! There have always been lots of girls around, but you didn't bother with them until the hormones kicked in."

"And when do your hormones kick in?"

Caleb couldn't help noticing the changes that were happening not only to their bodies, but to Jo's as well. Well, he always knew she was a girl but he considered her to be one of the guys for so long. Being a teenager seemed to be a confusing time. They were changing into adults, but were still children.

He found much of it frustrating. He was taller than his mother. He found that he no longer liked to wake up early in the morning. He was staying up later and sleeping in later on Saturday mornings. He didn't like it when his voice cracked and he would speak lower, then higher in the same sentence. He didn't like zits.

Caleb felt uncomfortable talking to his mother about the things that were happening to his body and would ask his father. He had been through the same things that he was going through now.

Jo splashed water at him to get his attention. "So are you gonna do it?"

"Uh? What are you talking about?"

Justin laughed. "Lose your cherry. What do you think she's talking about."

She stuck her tongue out at him. "You are so crude, Justin. I was not talking about that at all. Are you going to get baptized this summer?"

Justin groaned. "Come on guys, we are going to go to high school and all those hot babes and you want to talk church. Sheesh!"

Caleb laughed at his friend. He was never as interested in church as he and Jo were. He would go occasionally with them when he had nothing better to do. He always went to Vacation Bible School with them and would go at Christmas time to see his friends in the holiday program.

He looked back over at Jo. "I think so. It is important to do what Jesus commands us to do. How about you?"

Jo nodded. "You bet, wouldn't miss it for the world."

Justin shook his head at the two of them. "So when do you take the dip?"

"I'm not sure. Doc wants to meet with all of those who are interested in doing it. He is going to do a Bible study this week at prayer meeting."

Justin laughed. "I don't know. I thought I'd start with the football team. They are starting tryouts this weekend. Want to come, Jo? White is such a nerd. He wouldn't know what a football was."

"Ha, ha, ha." came the sarcastic reply. "I thought you would take up something more suited to your talents, like cleaning toilets."

They laughed, insulted each other and talked about what to expect until they pulled in at the small beach on the Jones' property. Alternately carrying and rolling the inner tubes, they hike up the trail through the trees to the farm.

Mrs. Jones had the barbeque smoking, waiting for those juicy hamburgers, hotdogs and sausages sitting in the fridge.

Justin's mother smiled at them as she watched them approach the house. "Did you have a nice time?" she said as she started to place the meet on the hot grill.

The three chorused yes's as they reached the picnic table and saw that she had also put out a big frosty pitcher of lemonade. She listened to them as they recounted the peaceful voyage on the lazy river.

As they gulped down the lemonade, Caleb's parents came around the corner of the house. Both were carrying salads for the barbeque. A few minutes later, Jo's parents drove up in their vehicle to join the party.

She ran over to them and gave them a big hug. Caleb would have liked to do the same thing to his parents, but that just wasn't a cool thing to do when you are a thirteen-year old guy; at least not in public.

Mr. White put the potato salad he was carrying on the table and moved to ruffle his son's hair. He caught Caleb's warning look, winked and dropped his hand. "Catch anything?"

"Dad we weren't fishing. We were tubing."

"I know, but there are more things to catch than fish."

Caleb wrinkled his brow. "Yeah, Dad. I saw a moose standing on the edge of the river but it moved when I leapt off the tube to tackle it with my bare hands."

Mr. White laughed and went over to shake Carol's hand and then the Collins' as they had by this time walked over to join the small party. The two men went over to the lawn chairs and sat down after they helped themselves to the lemonade on the table. Brenda White turned to Alice Collins. "How have you been? It has been quite a while since we last got together."

Jo's mother smiled. "It has been a rather busy summer."

Carol had brought out some appetizers and set them on the table. "Hi, Alice; Brenda. Glad you could make it. We are almost ready."

She hurried over to the smoking BBQ to check on the progress of the meat sizzling away on the grill. She flipped the burgers and slapped on a thick layer of sauce to finish them up.

A few minutes later she motioned to everyone. "Ok. It's time to eat!"

The teens filled their plates and then went to sit under a nearby willow tree. They quickly demolished what they had eaten and went back for seconds.

"Thank you for the meal," said Caleb. "It was delicious."

The ladies accepted the compliment and went back to the visiting. Justin, Caleb and Jo quickly picked up their paper plates, plastic cups and utensils and deposited them in the garbage can. They slipped away to the fort.

"How are we going to change?" asked Justin when they were in the cool green confines of the towering pine that had been their fort and refuge for the last five years.

Caleb was sitting on the lowest branch of the tree. "Well we all know you are going to get uglier than you are now."

Justin threw a stick at him and missed. "Listen dork face! Mom was saying that becoming a teenager is a big step as we grow up and learn to be independent. I mean, what are you looking forward to now that we will be going to a different school with different people?"

Caleb shrugged. "Can't tell you. I am wondering if I will make a lot of friends, if I will do ok in my classes. You know. That kind of stuff."

Jo, who was sitting at the base of the tree, looked up at him. "You will always do ok in your classes Caleb. You were the valedictorian of our graduating class."

Justin made a gagging noise as he pretended to stick his finger down his throat. "Come on you guys. It is a whole new world to explore. More freedom, do what you want. Have a good time."

"And just exactly what is your idea of a good time?" Jo asked.

Justin shrugged. "Not sure. But I have heard there is a lot of stuff that goes on. Wild parties on the weekend. Lots of weed to smoke. It all depends on getting in with the right crowd."

"But what if that crowd is not the right one? I don't know about all that stuff you're talking about. I'd rather find a group of Christian teens I can hang with." said Jo. "I really don't believe you are going to smoke weed or any other drug, Justin Jones. You are just saying that to see how much you can shock me."

"Yeah, right."

Caleb knew better. "Come on Justin, admit you like to get Jo all worked up so you can argue with her."

Justin sat up straighter, pretending to be offended. "I do not get Jo all worked up so I can argue with her. She just likes to argue with me, that's all."

She threw a pinecone at him. "You are a fruitcake. So, all talk, no action. Are you coming with us on Wednesday night to find out what's it all about?"

Justin looked over at his friends. "I'll think about it. But I'm not getting dunked even if I do."

Chapter Seventeen

Justin joined them Wednesday night for Bible study on baptism. Doc set up a white board and placed a stack of papers on the pulpit. "Hi, y'all," he drawled. "Since we are going to be spending a bit more time tonight then our usual prayer meeting, we are going to sing only a couple of songs and then two or three men pray."

After they had finished praying Doc picked up the papers and gave some to Caleb, Jo and Justin to hand out. "Ok, if you are here tonight, especially if it is not your habit to come to prayer meeting, then you must be interested in getting baptized."

He cleared his throat and took a sip of water from a glass he had set on the side of the pulpit. "First of all, let's talk about what baptism isn't."

He stood up and walked over to the white board, taking the cap off his marker as he moved. He wrote a number one on the board. "The first thing you should know is that water baptism does not wash away your sins. You're sins have been taken care of when Jesus died on the cross."

He wrote a number two. "Water Baptism does not save you nor is it necessary for your salvation. Jesus work on the cross was complete."

The number three joined the other two numbers. "Water baptism is not a sacrament that bestows grace upon you."

He added number four. "The method of baptism is not sprinkling, pouring or placing a mark in water on your forehead. The word means to immerse. We will take a closer look at that later on."

He turned to face his audience. "These are all misconceptions about what baptism is and does for you. When we examine what the Bible has to say about it, water baptism is an outward picture of an inward reality. I know that sounds puzzling at the moment, but hopefully we will clear that up by the end of the evening. If we need to, we can spend another week or two on this subject. Does anyone have any questions before we start?"

He paused. "Ok. So if you have any questions, please jot them down and we will deal with them during the course of our study."

"Let's turn our Bibles to Matthew twenty-eight verses nineteen and twenty. *"Go therefore and make disciples of all the nations, baptizing them in the name of the Father and of the Son and of the Holy Spirit, teaching them to observe all things that I have commanded you; and lo, I am with you always, even to the end of the age."* Amen.

He looked up from his Bible. "This is what we know as The Great Commission. We are commanded to make disciples of all nations and baptize those disciples, teaching them and training them to do the same thing."

The study took two more weeks to complete. By the end Caleb understood that baptism pictured the death, burial and resurrection into his new spiritual life. He learned baptism was a public declaration that he was a disciple of Christ.

He also discovered there was more than one baptism spoken of in the Bible which tended to cause some confusion. Caleb didn't know that when He was saved, the Holy Spirit place him or baptized him into the body of Christ. He discovered through the study John the Baptist baptized people who had repented and were looking forward to the coming of the Messiah.

On the last evening of the study, Doc explained to them what to expect and what to do. He demonstrated on a willing victim, Jo, how he would hold and support them while he was submersing them into the water.

"Now remember, I will be asking you a very important question. That question is I will ask you if you have received Jesus as your personal Savior. You will answer yes and then I will say, 'I baptize you in the name of the Father, and of the Son and of the Holy Spirit.' "

"Then you will hand me your handkerchief and hold your one hand on your other wrist. This will make a handy handle for me to use to lift you out of the water."

The participants gave a chuckle. "I will put my other arm behind you for the same reason. That way I won't leave you on the bottom of the river."

They agreed on the Sunday after the Labor Day weekend for the ceremony. The Sheppards, members of the chapel family, offered their house and yard for a church picnic and staging area for the baptism. They lived across from the public boat launch and dock. The water was not deep there and offered a good view for the people gathering to witness the event.

Caleb was excited about the baptism. Although he was a little apprehensive informing his parents about his decision. He felt this was an important step for him to take. He wanted to make a public declaration of his faith. He wanted to show them he was serious about his faith. But he had a week and half to discuss this with them. He didn't wanted to spring it on him the day of the event.

Icthus

Chapter Eighteen

Caleb was surprised by his parents' reaction to his decision to get baptized. They had never fully understood Caleb's interest in going to Church but felt that it wouldn't cause any harm. They had also hoped that by being involved in such an organization it would help him to make smart choices when he was older and would face peer pressure to engage in unsafe activities.

They made the twice yearly pilgrimage to the chapel at Christmas time and Easter in order to see their son in the programs. They even allowed him to attend the weekly Bible club as they also allowed him to participate in Scouts.

It was with great relief and happiness Caleb reported to Jo that his parents were going to attend and see him baptized. He wished that they would be standing with him in the water as Jo's parents were going to be. They became Christians in the months following the death of Jo's grandmother.

Alice and Bob Collins had been touched by the way the members of the chapel had reached out to their family because of their association with Jo. Members of the chapel had arranged for meals to be brought to them the week after the funeral. Doc had told them that the chapel was a family that looked out for each other. They were available to support Jo in any way she might need. That included visiting her family and helping them through the difficult and painful grieving process.

About two months after the death of Alice's mother, they called Doc and asked him to come over to their house. They had questions regarding what the chapel believed and wanted to discuss it with him. Doc answered their questions and presented the plan of salvation to them. When he invited them to accept Jesus offer of eternal life, they agreed to it and knelt with him in their living room.

The day of the baptism turned out to be a beautiful day. The sun was shining and the weather was considered hot for this part of the country for the time of year. Parents supervised their children as they splashed around in the water. Some of adults had also decided to go for a swim.

On the lawn of John and Taila Sheppard several portable tables had been set up. A makeshift salad bar had been built and was sitting on a couple of saw horses. The salad bar was a box lined with plastic and filled with ice to keep the salads cold. Coolers were filled with ice which kept bottles of pop, juice and water cold. Four barbeques were set up along the side of the lawn and several men were busy grilling the meats the families brought to the picnic.

After the people had finished eating and talking, they crossed the dirt road that separated the house from the river and the public dock. It was a small dock: only about four meters by two. It was designed to allow one or two smaller boats to pull up and tie off. To the side was a concrete ramp that led down into the water: the boat launch. Caleb looked down into the water. It was fairly shallow, only a few feet deep.

Doc motioned for people to gather around him. They formed in a semi-circle on the dock and along the road. "We are gathered here, not just to enjoy this fine day and all the good food we just finished consuming."

People smiled and nodded. "We are together to observe something which was commanded by Jesus. That was to make a public declaration of our allegiance to Him in the waters of baptism. It is not designed to give us salvation or God's grace but it is a sign of the new life He gave us when He provided His Son, Jesus Christ, who gave His life to give us life."

Icthus

He opened his Bible. "We read in Romans six, verses three and four: " ...*do you not know that as many of us as were baptized into Christ Jesus were baptized into His death? Therefore we were buried with Him through baptism into death, that just as Christ was raised from the dead by the glory of the Father, even so we also should walk in newness of life.*"

He moved his head as he spoke to the group gathered around him, trying to make eye contact with as many as possible. "These people have already been raised to a new life; a life that was bought with the blood of Jesus Christ. What we are seeing today is their public declaration of that spiritual reality."

He bowed his head. "Gracious and glorious Father, we come before you, your humble servants, to worship and praise you. Like our brethren who for nearly two millennia have done before us we desire to be obedient to your command to make disciples and to baptize them in the name of the Holy Trinity."

He paused for a moment, "May you bestow your blessing upon them as they take this step and publicly declare themselves as your disciples. May you always guide their footsteps and that they will glorify Your holy name. In Jesus name we give you praise, amen."

He raised his head and grinned. He handed his Bible to his wife and then walked over to the edge of the dock and jumped in. The water came up to his chest.

He moved out from the dock a few feet and then turned to face the people on the dock. He motioned for the first of the ones who had indicated their desire to be baptized.

There were eight in all. Justin decided that he would be baptized if just to shut up Jo and Caleb. He went into the water with Caleb and Doc asked the important question to which Caleb laughed and said "Yes!" Justin merely nodded. The people clapped and cheered as doc leaned them back into the water and back out again. They made their way to the dock and the people on it helped them out of the water.

Jo stood in the water with her parents. All three of them had decided to take a public stand as a family. Caleb, now standing on the deck wrapped in a towel stood between his parents as they watch the rite. He cheered and clapped with the rest of the people when they had been baptized as well.

The rest of the candidates had also been baptized and Doc was left standing in the water. "If there is anyone who is standing here today has come to the conviction Jesus Christ is indeed the answer God has provided for your sins, you can accept this gift of salvation right now and come down here to publicly declare your choice."

Caleb missed the look that passed between his parents. David White squeezed his son's shoulder and he looked at him. It surprised Caleb that he was almost as tall as his father. "Son, your mother and I thank-you for the huge child's size faith you have in Jesus. After you pleaded your case to be baptized we called and met the Doc. He was very straightforward and persuasive in his arguments."

To Caleb's total amazement, his parents walked to the edge of the dock and jumped in. The water swirled about them as they made their way to where Doc stood. A big grin on his face as he winked at Caleb. "This is a surprise for Caleb today folks. As you know he's constantly asked for prayer over the last three or four years that his parents would come to know Jesus and accept him as their savior. Son, your faithful prayers have been answered.

 He looked at Mr. White. "David, do you acknowledge Jesus Christ to be your personal Lord and Savior?"

"I openly declare that I have accepted Jesus Christ to be my Lord and Savior."

Caleb could feel the tears coursing down his face.

Doc then turned and asked the same thing of his mother. "I believe that Jesus Christ died for my sins and is the Lord of my life."

Jo danced over to Caleb and gave him a big hug. Doc held up his hand. "David and Brenda, based on the confession of your faith before these witnesses, I baptize the both of you in the name of the Father, the Son and the Holy Spirit."

Caleb cheered louder than everyone. He was so happy. His parents were going to Heaven with him. They came to the ladder at the dock side and climbed up it, his mother first and then his father.

Doc, smiling, winked at Caleb. "The gift of God is free to all anytime. Is there anyone else who would like to publicly declare their faith?"

He waited for a minute or two before heading towards the dock.

He climbed out to shake hands and hug the candidates who were also being bombarded with hugs and handshakes from the rest of the people standing on the dock.

With the baptisms over, the children jumped into the water again while the adults made their way back to the lawn to indulge in more desserts and to visit before going their separate ways.

Icthus

Chapter Nineteen

Life in the White home changed after that special September afternoon. His parents started attending services with him and they became very interested in the Book he had been learning about since he was nine years old.

Where they would get up and get ready for work, they now started a routine of morning devotions. Doc had started a training program, teaching people the basics of their faith. He, his parents and the Collins took advantage of these sessions and often took turns hosting them in their homes.

By the time Caleb turned sixteen, both his dad and Mr. Collins were recognized as deacons and were active in taking care of chapel maintenance and working to help meet needs of the members that arose. Mrs. White, also active in the life of the chapel, started to teach Sunday school, although not Caleb's age group. The unique ministry of dealing with the angst of teenagers was left to the very capable Mr. James, who had been working with the youth for several years.

He and Jo started dating but were very casual about it. Both boys had made the football team and in the spring Caleb went out for the track and field and had been successful in competitions with the other high schools.

Caleb knew the Lord had been good to him but there were a few wrinkles in his life. He was becoming more concerned about Justin. His childhood buddy had never been overly interested in attending church with them or many of the church-sponsored activities, such as the Friday night youth group. He was more interested in the girls, going to the monthly dances and the parties at school chums' houses every few weeks.

He suspected Justin was or may still be using marijuana and maybe a few other drugs. Whenever he broached the subject with him, Justin would laugh and change the subject. Caleb found it hard to see the road his friend seemed determined to travel.

"How can you tell me that this stuff is bad for me when you have never tried it yourself?" he would use as a rebuttal against Caleb.

"Justin, you don't have to drink rat poison to know it's bad for you. There is a cross and skull right on the bottle."

It was late spring of that year when Caleb learned that his friend had tried something else.

Justin had been talking about Lucy. She was a red-haired girl that had a reputation around the school. The kind of reputation most boys like and most girls think is not a good thing. He told Caleb that he had a date with her.

When he asked where they were going, Justin replied that he was talking her on a picnic on top of The Bluffs. "Do you think that's a good idea?" he asked his friend. "Being alone with a girl in a place like that."

Justin laughed. "Don't be such a wet blanket. I'm taking her on a picnic not to a hotel room."

Justin didn't need a hotel room. A picnic on The Bluffs was all it took. Lucy's reputation was well deserved. Justin had wondered why he had waited so long to experience the delights of a woman. But then he knew the answer. He had always been influenced by his close friendship with Caleb and Jo. He had widened his circle of friends and acquaintances considerably since starting high school.

It irritated him that Caleb had put the pieces together so easily. He did experiment with drugs and alcohol. He didn't care for the aftereffects and decided not to indulge in them a great deal. Some of his friends did smoke weed and he would sometimes spend a Saturday night toking with them.

He didn't understand what the big deal was. Jo and Caleb took it upon themselves to act as his conscience. He was never interested in the church scene as they were. He was baptized with them because he was their friend and they had kept pestering him to join them.

He lied when he said he was a Christian. He never made that commitment and had no interest in doing so. In spite of their prudishness, he liked hanging out with them. They were a comfortable habit.

Justin found a whole new level of freedom when he obtained his driver's license. He was no longer dependent on mom to drive him where he wanted to go. It allowed him to go on dates; like the one he recently had with Lucy. He planned to go on more dates like that.

He lay on his bed and laced his fingers behind his head. He had on headphones, listening to his favorite heavy metal band. He bobbed his head and tapped his toes to the beat. His eyes were closed and he was mouthing the words. He was sixteen, closer to seventeen now. He had the whole world before him and he wanted to experience it all!

He wasn't sure at this point what he wanted to do when he graduated from high school. His mother got on his case about starting to plan and consider what he would like to pursue as a career.

He already knew that he wasn't interested in academics. He didn't care for books and spending time in stuffy classrooms. He thought of Caleb's interest in the new field of computers. His friend would spend hours working on programming problems and had even taken electronics courses to help him better understand this new technology.

A section of the White's basement had been given over to this fascination with computers. A workbench filled with tools and electronic circuitry littered the table. Caleb said they would change the world as we know it.

Justin thought that was extremely possible this might be the case in the future. But that was something that also did not interest him. Technical details like that would drive him crazy. But he had over eighteen months before a he was required to make any solid decisions.

He made up his mind long before that deadline was on the horizon. They attended a job/education fair during his senior year. He was walking with Jo and Caleb among the booths with the different companies and schools which were working to entice these young people to apply.

The armed forces booth attracted Justin and he spoke with the recruiting officer.

Being a fan of action movies, he was intrigued with the idea of going into Black Ops. Undercover stuff that nobody talked about, but everyone knew existed.

The recruiting officer showed Justin several brochures and laughed when he asked about it. "Well, it's not called Black Ops, but there are certainly similar military careers if you qualify for them."

He pulled his brief case out from under the table and rifled through it. He pulled out three more army career brochures and handed them to Justin. They described the Canadian Special Operations Regiment, 427 Special Operations Aviation Squadron and the Canadian Joint Incident Response Unit.

Justin also discovered he could enlist right out of high school. If he wanted to pursue a college education, then the military would pay for his training in exchange for extra years of service on his contract.

The recruiter indicated to Justin that a military career was a win-win situation. He would get what he wanted in the pursuit of his goals and the country would get a loyal and dedicated protector.

Caleb was drawn to the schools that were offering computer technology programs. Jo looked at teaching or nursing options. "Hey, Collins! You gonna become a nurse?" said Justin.

She made a face at him. "I'm going to go to Bible College first and then I'll decide what I want to pursue after that. God hasn't indicated a direction for me to follow yet."

"Bible College? Isn't that a waste of time? Unless you're gonna become a preacher?"

Caleb looked over at him. "No. It is important to have a good foundation to build your life on. A solid year or two to get grounded and then off to secular college or university to train in the field you want to pursue unless God has other plans."

Justin looked at his friend with a new light. "Are you considering going to one instead of that computer engineering program you keep going on about?"

Caleb nodded. "Yes, I am thinking about doing that. It means an extra year or two of school, but I think that is what God is leading me to do. Are you serious about the army?"

Justin shrugged. "I don't have the brain power you do and the idea of another four years of school doesn't appeal to me at all. I suppose I could go into a trade, but the military will train me in any area I want to go in and it won't cost anything."

They were sitting down at a table in the food court in the mall across the street from the center where the fair was going on. Jo was picking at her fries, dipping them in ketchup and then slowly chewing them. "I think I would prefer to go to a smaller school than a larger one."

Caleb took a swig on his chocolate shake. "I'm pretty sure I can get scholarships for the schools I want to attend. I have the grades to get it. But I am planning on going to the Bible Institute in Parry Sound first."

Justin and Jo looked at him thoughtfully. The school had a year-long program that included not only academic study but practical as well. For the past several years the organization had, at the invitation of the chapel, sent its musical group to a weekend winter retreat for teenagers.

Jo swallowed and took a sip of her diet Coke. "That sounds like a cool idea. I had been thinking of going to a three or four year place, but you can get two years credit for the one year there, correct?"

Caleb nodded as he took a big bite of his burger. As soon as he had swallowed it he said, "Yeah. I like the idea that they have practical stuff for you to do as well. The opportunity to put into practice what you preach is appealing to me. I don't want to spend all that time learning stuff and not being able to use it until after graduation."

Justin had heard enough preachy stuff for one day. "So did you hear about the party this weekend at Pine's? I hear it is gonna be a wild night. His parents have gone on vacation." He grinned at them over his coke. "No supervision! Whatya say?"

Caleb looked over at his friend. "You already know the answer to that one. You talked me into one of these parties last spring. My answer is, 'been there, done that.'"

"Whatever."

"You have no interest in attending Bible College at all, Justin?" Asked Jo.

"Nah, like I said, I am not into books and all that cerebral stuff. I'm bored with school. I want action."

"Your mom is not gonna like that at all. We all know how big she is on your getting a good education."

Justin shrugged. "It's my life. And besides I am still getting an education, just not by sitting in a classroom all day for the next four years."

Justin knew Caleb suspected the truth about him. More than once he had questioned how his friend could in all conscience carry on in the activities he was pursuing when he claimed to be a Christian.

He usually managed to deflect the point Caleb was attempting to make. He hardly showed his face in church and rarely involved himself in church life. His decision had put a strain on the long friendship he had with Jo and Caleb but it had not been pushed to the breaking point.

Today he was sipping drinks, munching burgers and fries with his oldest and best friends. Tonight he would be partying with his other set of friends. The ones not hung up on religion.

Icthus

Chapter Twenty

"So in conclusion, fellow grads, a chapter in our lives comes to an end. But this is cause for celebration. We have taken another step to adulthood. The next chapter is about to begin. It is a fresh start filled with possibilities. Thank you."

Caleb stood at the podium while his graduating peers threw their caps into the air and cheered. The guests behind them clapped vigorously. He wished the ceremony was over, but there was still closing remarks by the principal and the recessional of them marching out of the auditorium while flashbulbs went off as proud parents, relatives and friends snapped pictures of the auspicious occasion.

He was dying to get this silly robe off of him and head for home, but he knew that wasn't about to happen. He gave his parents a big hug and then the Collins and finally Mrs. Jones. He stood and smiled with them in a similar order while their picture was taken.

Jo ran up to him and threw her arms about him. Justin sauntered up and punched him in the arm. They stood, with their arms around each other, while their parents snapped away. They had survived to graduate high school.

"Hey, White." laughed Justin. "Two for two, what are you, Mr. Valedictorian where ever you go?"

Caleb grimaced. "It's not my fault that I have brains and a personality to boot. Not to mention the good looks. Too bad for you."

Jo rolled her eyes. "Puleeze! Not too conceited are we?"

She looked over to Justin. "Are you coming to the church reception this weekend or do you have to leave right away for boot camp?"

Justin made up his mind and paid a visit to the local recruiting office a few weeks after he turned eighteen. He would be leaving in a week for Petawawa to begin his military career. "Well at least I will be drawing a regular pay check. How many years ahead to do you have before you can say that?"

Caleb had been right all those months ago about Justin's mother's reaction to him wanting to go into the military instead of pursuing an educational path. They had several arguments, but he would not be swayed. She may have been unhappy but had come to terms with the fact her son had grown up and was capable of making his own decisions.

She stood smiling and laughing with the rest of them that warm June day.

Caleb and Jo had both decided to attend the year long term at the Parry Sound Bible Institute. Their decision had the blessing of their parents. It also had the blessing of the Elders of North Woods Bible Chapel. They had grown up in the Assembly and the extended family which assisted them on their spiritual journey.

Caleb knew Justin would go this route. They had talked about the future a great deal in the months leading up to this day. He attempted several times to change Justin's mind, to join them at the institute instead. "It's only for a year. You're telling me you can't join the army next year instead of this year?"

For nostalgic reasons they met at the now abandoned fort. The stately pine still stood, but as they had moved from childhood towards adulthood, the food court at the mall became the new place to hang out.

Justin sighed. "Have you been talking to my mom again, White? We have had this discussion before. I am not interested in going to school - any school, period. It is not because it's a Bible College, although I doubt Mom would approve of that any more than my decision to go into the army."

Caleb had to concede that point. Brenda Jones had never shown much interest in spiritual things until recently. When his mother or Mrs. Collins invited her to various ladies functions, she would use the excuse she had to work. Correction, Caleb thought. She showed no interest in Christian spiritual things. What did interest Brenda Jones was the emerging spiritual movement called the New Age.

She accepted her son's decision, not that she could stop it, considering he was an adult in the eyes of the government. Caleb was positive that she viewed the army as the lesser of two evils.

"You presented her with a done deal. She really didn't have any choice in the matter. She is all you've got and she has visions of you coming home in a box."

"Ah, come on, White, I'm going to live forever."

"Really? On whose say so?"

"I like what Paul said, 'eat, drink, and be merry, for tomorrow we die.'"

Caleb shook his head. "That's not exactly what he said and you know enough to realize that you ripped that so totally out of context."

Justin sat up and looked directly at his friend. "We have been buds most of our short lives. I love you like the brother I never had. But I have to do this. I wish you understood and respected my decision."

Caleb did understand all too well. "It is like my conviction that I need to spend this coming year at the Bible Institute."

Justin threw a handy pine cone at his friend. "You need to go there because Jo is going there." He saw Caleb start to shake his head. "Don't give me that God is directing you crap. Your hormones are directing you to go there instead of to a real school."

"Actually we arrived at our decisions to go there separately. But I'm glad we are going to the same place, at least for this coming year. After that who knows?"

Justin leaned back against the tree again. "Come on, man, admit it, she has you by the short hairs."

Caleb blushed. "I will admit no such thing." But he was smiling all the same.

Chapter Twenty-one

It was the final Sunday Caleb and Jo would be with the Assembly for a while. They would be leaving that week to go to the Bible institute. He was sitting with Jo in the auditorium for the first meeting, called the Lord's Supper or Communion.

Caleb always appreciated this service. There was no chairman, preacher or worship leader. People shared a thought, a passage of Scripture or requested a song as they felt led to do so by the Holy Spirit. At the front on the table sat a cup of wine and a loaf of bread. Usually, after about 45 minutes, one of the men would give thanks for the bread, then go up and break the loaf. It would be passed from person to person: each breaking off a piece and eating it. Then someone would give thanks for the cup and pass it around as well.

This simple act of remembrance was commanded by Christ the night before He was crucified. Caleb came to understand this was the sign of the New Covenant which the prophet Jeremiah had written about over five hundred years before Jesus was even born.

There was a break between the first meeting and the family Bible hour. Chapel members visited with each other, sipping coffee, tea or juice and munching on cookies provided by the ladies of the Assembly. Five minutes before the next meeting someone rang a warning bell. People quickly drained their cups and started back to the auditorium.

The worship team started to play as stragglers hurried to their seats. John White was chairing the meeting today and was welcoming everyone. The words appeared on a screen beside him and he motioned for people to stand and sing.

The speaker today was Doc. He smiled out at the audience. "Today is a bittersweet day as we bid goodbye to a couple of our children, now adults. There is some sadness as they will not be with us for a while, but we are excited because they are following where God wants them to be."

"After the message, I will call Caleb and Jo up here along with the other Elders. We will lay hands on them and commend them to their studies and ask the Lord's blessing."

"So my message today is appropriately located in Second Timothy two, verse fifteen: '*Be diligent to present yourself approved to God, a worker who does not need to be ashamed, rightly dividing the word of truth.*'"

Caleb only paid half attention to the message today. His thoughts were with Justin. He had heard almost nothing from his friend since he left for basic training the week after grad. He had hoped Justin would have reconsidered his enrollment in the military until he had grounded himself by going to the Bible institute with them for the year.

Caleb had his suspicions about Justin. He never showed much interest in spiritual things. His actions during high school were not consistent with a person who would claim to be a Christian. Sure he knew other church kids as well who sometimes acted like Justin did, but there was always something about Justin's attitude that concerned him.

He prayed regularly for Justin, that he would find a good church home where he was. Caleb knew that he should be finished his basic training shortly and might even come home on furlough before starting the next round of training.

He wouldn't get to touch base with him even if he came home. Caleb would be at the Bible Institute and wasn't planning on coming home until the Christmas break.

Jo elbowed him in the side. He was lost in thought and realized the Elders were up at the front looking at them. He realized that they were ready to lay hands on them and commend them to their future endeavors.

Blushing, he stood up and hurried up to the platform with Jo. The Elders gathered around them and Doc began to pray. "Heavenly Father, we thank you for Your gracious mercy that you continually bestow upon us. We thank you for the lives of these two young people who have committed themselves to following you. As they step out on this new part of their journey, we pray for your blessing upon them. That their faithfulness to your Son and their desire to learn more about you and your word will help them grow and prepare for a life of ministry. We thank-you once again. In your Son's precious name. Amen."

Caleb opened his eyes and blinked. He looked up and over to Jo and prepared to make a bee line back to his seat. Doc reached out and grabbed his arm. "Whoa, not so fast, there."

He gave a puzzled look to the old pastor, who was grinning from ear to ear. "To help you and Jo," Caleb could see that Doc had grabbed her arm too. "The Chapel is giving you one thousand dollars to help with school expenses."

The members of the assembly whistled, clapped and cheered. Doc leaned over to Caleb. "Er... you can close your mouth, you know. You're not catching flies."

He swallowed and looked over at Jo, who was just as dumbfounded. He turned and faced the audience once more. "I am truly humbled by your generous gift and support. I pray that I will not let you down."

Jo was more succinct. "What he said."

People laughed as they rushed down the steps of the platform and headed back to their seats. People were reaching out to shake their hands as they passed. Several stood up and gave them hugs. They finally made it back to their seats and a few minutes later Doc concluded the morning's service with an invitation to move to the fellowship hall to enjoy the going away potluck; the delicious odors wafting through the building and teasing the congregation for the past hour.

People quickly stood up and gathered their belongings. Several more made their way over to the couple to congratulate them and wish them well in their studies. They chatted as they made their way to the fellowship hall and by now, were not that surprised to see a big banner with their names on it. As the guests of honor, they were first in line at table, loaded down with all the standard dishes they would normally find at a potluck.

They sat down at one of the long tables and started to eat. Jo nudged him and motioned for him to look up. On the projection screen was a slide show showing them from the time they were babies to their activities as children going to the chapel. He gave his parents a dirty look.

Apparently the Assembly wasn't above roasting them some more. He grimaced and grinned at Jo, who appeared just as uncomfortable by the show. They understood this was all done with the best of intentions and decided to roll with the punches. The day would soon be over and their attention would be focused on the many tasks they had to complete before they left for Parry Sound by the end of the week.

Chapter Twenty-two

The first thing that Justin felt that Sunday morning was the massive headache of a hangover. Graduation from basic had been the day before and his fellow graduates partied long into the night. He opened his eyes and winced at the light coming from the window.

He slowly swung his feet around and placed them on the floor and flinched when they made contact with the cold tiles. Carefully he stood up and staggered over to his locker. He reached into it and blindly searched for the bottle of Tylenol. Struggling with the child proof cap, he finally tore the lid off and tipped the bottle, capturing two pills in his hand which he immediately tossed into his mouth and swallowed them.

Justin made his way to the latrine where he relieved himself before shuffling back to his bed. He heaved a sigh of relief as he lay back down. Man that was some party, he thought. Every muscle and bone in his body ached. It felt a little like his first week at camp.

Being an independent person, he at first resented having all say in his life taken away. They told him when to get up (He had stayed up till four in the morning, but never got up at that time.), what he would eat and when (The food was so-so, but plentiful.) and what he would wear. The days had been long with numberless drills from physical education to handling weapons.

Towards the end of the training, he embraced the way the military worked. He set the pace for his fellow platoon members. During the week he excelled at the proper care of his gear. He could take apart and reassemble his rifle faster than any of his mates. He pushed them as they ran the miles and did countless pushups and other exercises designed to strip them of their civilian softness and mold them into efficient soldiers.

He had succeeded in completing the training. He worked long and hard and earned top honors in his platoon. His Commanding Officer was pleased with him. "Private, you are one of the finest examples of a soldier we have seen come through here in a long while."

He had made Platoon leader during his time and caught the attention of the brass. It looks like he was one step closer to reaching his goal of joining Special Ops. A week before graduation he sat down with his platoon sergeant to discuss the next step of his military career. "Well, Jones." Sargent Michaels flipped through his file. He looked up at Justin. "It looks like you are going to go places."

"Yes, Sargent."

"Your initial assessment indicated your desire to go into Special Operations. Is that correct?"

"Yes, Sargent."

"Well, I have seen nothing in the past few months that indicate why you can't move towards your goal. It is not an easy career path."

"No, Sargent. I wasn't expecting it to be."

"The dropout rate for this path is upwards of eighty per cent. Only the most determined and best of our troops make it."

"Yes, Sargent."

"How would you like to take a small detour before you enter the Special Ops field?"

Justin looked puzzled for the first time. "Sargent?"

"I see real leadership potential in you. So does Captain Philips. He wants you to consider attending the Officers school before you start your specific training."

Justin's eyebrows climbed in surprise. "I wasn't expecting this."

Sargent Michaels smiled and nodded. "Well, at least not this early in your career, eh Jones? You could eventually get there this route, but the highest you can go as an enlisted man is Chief Warrant Officer. Which is a great goal to achieve but you already know that. Eventually you would have to go through the officers' training if you wanted to advance further."

"We don't make this offer to just anyone. You have already distinguished yourself with your commanding officers and they see the potential in you to succeed at whatever you decide to do with your military career. Your performance has opened doors for you that don't open for just anybody."

Justin sat quietly as he digested the words Sargent Michaels had just spoken. "Such an honor could go to a guy's head, Sargent."

He leaned back in his chair and laughed. "And you are sure you won't let it go to your head, Jones?"

Justin grinned. "Well, just a bit."

"Look. It's a big decision on which way to go. You will end up as an officer eventually anyway. Your talent and determination will not go unnoticed for long. There are openings in both schools. Take a day or two to think about it and get back to me. You are dismissed."

Justin stood up and saluted, then reached out and shook the Sargent's hand. "Thank-you, sir."

Nine days later he lay in bed waiting for the hangover to ease off. Of course he decided to go through the officers' training first. He would be a fool not to.

The Sargent made him aware the rank would make no difference when he entered special operations training. All personnel were treated the same during the initial training process. It did not matter if you were a corporal or a lieutenant, your trainers ranked you during your time with them. They were the gods in your life, determining if you would reach your goals or not. Justin was determined he was going to reach his goals.

Chapter Twenty-three

Caleb stood on the platform, the podium in front of him. He wasn't expecting to be addressing his graduating class. He and Jo had a good chuckle about it when they found out. "What is it about you that you always get to be the valedictorian?" asked Jo as they were relaxing on their day off from a week of teen campers.

"It's probably my irresistible good looks and charm," he replied, innocently looking up at the ceiling.

Jo threw a seat cushion at him, the only thing she had handy at the moment. "You conceited jack ass!"

The cushion hit him in the face. "Whoa, I am not. I can't help it if people like me. Too bad you have to work at it."

She gave an outraged gasp and launched herself at him, tickling his sides. He was laughing so hard he wasn't able to effectively fight her off. "Hey, what happened to the no physical contact rule?"

Jo by now had wrestled Caleb off the couch and was straddling his chest. "It doesn't apply to inflated egos."

She bent over him and leaned closer, her lips moving closer to his. He was going to like this. She then sat up and gave him a slap. "Now the no physical contact rule goes into effect."

She moved to get off of him. He made his move and heaved his body over, trapping her on the rug on the floor. "Now we will see about breaking that rule."

She was giggling. "I doubt it. Mrs. Carslyle has been watching us for the last five minutes."

Mrs. Carslyle was the Dean of Women at the Bible Institute. She guarded the girls as fiercely as a eunuch guarded the Sultan's harem from interlopers. He glanced up and sure enough, she was standing by the doorway. She had her arms crossed and was tapping one of her feet. "Mr. White, if I hadn't witnessed the few minutes before, you would be in serious trouble."

Caleb stood up and reached down to help Jo stand up. "Yes, ma'am. For what it's worth, I didn't start this. She just can't keep her hands off me."

Jo turned and gave him a punch on the arm. He winced and rubbed the spot. Mrs. Carslyle shook her head as she tried to keep the smile off her face. "I highly doubt that Mr. White. It's a good thing there are no campers here. I won't say carry on. Now behave yourselves, graduation is only a week and a half away."

Both Caleb and Jo mumble. "Yes, ma'a'm." Looking at each other and smiling.

It had been a busy and challenging year. On the first day they were assigned ministry duties, either singing in the school's choir, ministering in local churches or at the youth shelter. Tuesdays-Fridays were classroom days. One class was in module format as a guest lecturer would come and spend two weeks with them. The other three classes were the length of the quarter and taught by staff.

Caleb, who grew up in a Bible believing church, realized how little he actually knew about the Bible. His mind was challenged constantly, stretching to accommodate new concepts or build upon the ones he already knew.

He was also challenged to step out more in ministry. At home, ministry opportunities were more if the person felt like doing something. Here it was required. He was terrified when he had learned that part of his training included street evangelism.

The week before Thanksgiving, the entire student body relocated to Toronto where they spent the week street preaching, singing, drawing or acting out the Gospel message. They spent the week before learning how to open air preach and share with people. The staff had lots of ideas and tips on how to speak to people about the Lord.

Caleb had butterflies in his stomach when they left that Monday to go to the provincial capital for the street outreach. He thought he would have a nervous breakdown before the first day was out. But he surprised himself and found that he enjoyed speaking with total strangers about their need for a Savior.

By the end of the week, he was hooked and disappointed the street evangelism was over. He was always hesitant to speak to strangers at all, keeping mostly to himself. When he was forced to do it, he found out it wasn't all that bad.

The rest of the quarter went by quickly. He excelled in his studies and was carrying a 4.0 when Christmas Break rolled around.

The winter quarter had its challenges as well. Every weekend for eight straight weeks, the institute hosted youth retreats. Each Friday evening over a hundred excited teens would descend on the institute.

The retreats would be a series of speakers with messages designed for teens and full slate of winter activities. The Saturday evening was one of the main attractions. After the speaker, they sang and held an activity called Body Life. The teens were placed into groups. On Saturday evening the group required to perform a skit, a song or other activity in a talent show. Caleb worked as a counselor each session, taking control of eight to ten rambunctious teen age boys.

Sunday morning was devoted to another worship session and the final attempt the speaker had to capture the teens' attention with vital spiritual challenges. The officially ended after lunch on Sunday.

The faculty and students would have the evening off as well as their usual Mondays. The retreats were in addition to their normal class load and other commitments.

By the time Spring Break rolled around, Caleb was very glad to have a breather. The Spring Quarter was more normal, But towards the end of the quarter, they were preparing for the summer quarter, which consisted of two solid months of operating summer camps.

Kids from eight to eighteen would be in these camps. The students were assigned tasks from house and grounds keeping to counseling and ministry teams.

Caleb had been assigned to the counseling team and would spend his summer working directly with the kids. He would be responsible for a group of boys every week. He would serve as their guide, counselor and warden if need be. He would live in the cabin with them and be there to direct their activities or to offer spiritual advice.

Although he had a tough assignment, he did not envy Jo who was on the ministry team. They would be responsible for the programs and teaching sessions held throughout the camp sessions. They had to learn several skits and practice every day, except Sunday to prepare for each week.

But they survived. Now Caleb was standing at the podium preparing to address his peers. Even he thought that was rather ironic; three for three commencement speeches. He looked out over the people gathered to help celebrate this passage in their lives. He could see his parents, Mr. and Mrs. Collins and a handful of people from North Woods Chapel.

During Christmas and quarter breaks he gave an update to the Chapel family and expressed his gratitude for their support both emotionally, spiritually and occasionally financially.

"Dear Friends: I know this is a little informal for such a formal event, but in the past year, you, my peers have become friends. No, more than that; you are part of an extended family that has existed for almost two thousand years. I for one have been very gratefully to get to know.

"We are gathered here today to mark another milestone in our lives. Whether it is your first graduation ceremony, or your fifth, or your tenth, it marks the completion of a goal that each one of us set out to accomplish. But it is a goal that we did not have to travel alone.

"The faculty and staff guided and assisted us as we struggled to understand new concepts and how to put them into practice. They challenged and stretched us to leave our comfort zones and take those steps of faith that God wants us to take. Hebrews eleven six states: *'But without faith it is impossible to please Him, for he who comes to God must believe that He is, and that He is a rewarder of those who diligently seek Him.'*

"We seek to please our Lord and Savior. That takes faith - a faith that is richly rewarded by the blessings of God. We learned through our studies that the road to please God is not always the easy path. He tests us and burns away the unnecessary until we are capable and fit for His Will.

"Paul wrote to Timothy: *'Be diligent to present yourself approved to God, a worker who does not need to be ashamed, rightly dividing the word of truth.'* Some Bibles use the word 'study' but the idea is to work hard. The goal is to be approved to God. It is not just gaining God's approval, but the idea that you have been tested and tried, much like the smelting process of gold. In the end the product is something that will stand in God's favor."

He paused and surveyed the crowd again and smiled. "Where would we be without the support of those who believed in us: our parents, family members, church families, and friends? It is truly a great blessing and privilege to stand here before you. It is an honor to have been chosen by my peers to address you today.

"However, it would not be proper for me to be the only one to say thank-you as we prepare to start a new chapter in our lives."

He motioned for his fellow graduates to come up to the platform once again. The 55 graduates jostled and joked until they were all on the small stage. Jason counted to three and they shouted out "THANK YOU!"

The audience clapped and stood up, cheering the graduating class. Classmates cheered and threw their mortarboards into the air. They laughed and hugged each other. When it had quieted down, Caleb grinned into the microphone. "Enough said. Time to part... er eat!"

The students filed back to their seats and the President of the Bible Institute came to the microphone. He shook his head and smiled. "Well, that was a little unorthodox for a valedictorian speech, but then I understand Caleb is an old hand at giving them."

He held up three fingers and silently mouthed the word three. "It wouldn't surprise me if I hear that he addresses the students of future graduating exercise he participates in.

"Caleb is correct. Now that the boring ceremonial stuff is over, it is time to party!

"Let's be dismissed in a word or two of prayer and we will adjourn to the banquet hall."

Chapter Twenty-four

Justin sat with his back to the cool stone wall. He could feel cold sweat on his face. His hands were shaking. There was blood on them. He was almost sure it wasn't his own.

His knife, also coated with blood, lay in the dirt at his feet. He took deep breaths to calm his nerves. His Commanding Officer hunkered down beside him. "This is your first kill?"

Justin looked at the other man and nodded. Captain Smith nodded grimly. "It will not get any easier. This is a part of our job as covert agents. We do what we have to do in order to survive and complete the mission. Jones, it was you or him. Do you understand that?"

He nodded again. He could feel his heart start to slow down as the adrenaline burned out of his system. "Did you feel this way when you first killed someone?"

The captain nodded. "You actually did better. I puked for three days afterward."

Justin gave a small smile. "You are trained in weapons tactics and you shoot and kill stuffed dummies, but it really doesn't prepare you for the real thing, does it?"

"No. All your training does is drill the instinct into you so that you react automatically without thinking. And that is what you did. You responded to the threat the way you were trained to do so."

"Lieutenant, this is one of the hardest assignments we have in the military. We technically do not exist and only the top one per cent is ever considered for this duty. Our mission is and always will be to work behind the scenes.

"Have you ever watched that old television show Mission Impossible?" Justin nodded. "Well we are them in real life. If we are caught, our government denies that we even exist. We are ghosts. We do what normal military and government channels are unable or unwilling to do.

"There are no heroes' welcomes for you, no parades, and no official commendations. But our world will sleep safer tonight because of what we do."

Captain Smith straightened slightly to peer over the top of stone wall. "It's clear, and we still have to get out of here. If you need to talk more, let's wait until we get back to the base."

Justin nodded. Now was not the time to sit down over a cup of coffee. They were still in enemy territory. Although they had accomplished their objectives, they still had to get out undetected and make it to the extraction point.

He was unnerved by this night's results, but he had trained for this moment for five years. That included a stint at the Royal Military College where he took the necessary courses he needed to obtained his commissioned status.

Still, it was the after classroom instruction that was the most challenging. He was trained in intelligence gathering, special weapons use, and espionage. He learned how to become a shadow, how to plant bugs, tap phones, hack into computer systems and harvest data.

He laughed at that last part. He hated computers. He had always found them boring, a means to an end. Caleb would also get a good laugh out the fact he was proficient enough in their usage to be able to hack them.

He learned other valuable tools as well: methods of extracting information from people. The world called it torture. They called it intelligence gathering.

He discovered most of these people who secretly served their country were hard core. They lived every moment in the present. They worked hard and partied hard. They knew that every mission could be their last mission. They faced the very real possibilities of capture or death. They also knew the likelihood of a burial at home would be remote to non-existent.

Justin was taught the art of subterfuge and each of them had lives outside of their real lives. Lives designed to deceive people into thinking they were logisticians, administrators or some other innocuous nine to five job on the base. They were drilled in the cover stories. The covers were never broken.

Mrs. Jones, who had always worried over her son's involvement in the military, was mollified that her son was in a safe job on a military base and that he would not have to face danger as long as the country was not involved in active military action. He had a desk job and that was fine with her.

Justin worked closely with his mentors and guides. He was a quick understudy becoming a valued member of the team. Captain Smith had been in covert operations for most of his military career. He took special interest in Justinand made him his unofficial apprentice.

Training was rigorous. He was tested to his limits, physically and mentally, and then beyond. He was put through a battery of psychological tests to determine his suitability to the program. There were times when he was bone weary and in pain and was required to push through it to complete the exercise.

When he wasn't being challenged to his physical limits, he was learning how to listen to conversations to determine what wasn't said. He became adept at the use of a variety of weapons, and what could be turned into one if the need arose.

He learned arts of warfare that weren't taught in any standard military classroom. It was nearly three years before he would be allowed to go on away missions which were considered strictly intelligence gathering.

He monitored the actions of the team on their missions and assisted in guiding them to their objectives. He took control of the targets computer systems and manipulated them to give his team a tactical advantage.

As his proficiency increased with weapons and guerilla tactics, his mission status changed in scope to hunting and capturing enemies of the state. He quickly learned that these enemies were not merely within the borders of Canada.

Even though he lived the pretense of an administrative assistant to Captain Smith, he was on-call twenty-four seven for any mission that arose: missions which had the potential send him anywhere in the world with when the phone rang.

He would be posted to overseas bases for short tours; a pretense for his real work. The mission he was on now was the third such one. It was the first time he was required to defend himself from an attacker.

They had infiltrated the compound of a known terrorist in Jordan. The objective of the mission was to locate this person and neutralize him. The captain took point. Justin was on left flank. They succeeded in entering the compound undetected. Their intelligence had placed the target there along with his seconds.

The place was well guarded, but the team had been able to meet their objective. They were extracting themselves when a guard spotted one of the team and had started to raise the alarm.

He ran towards them, raising his rifle and preparing to fire. Justin, who was the closest to the guard, jumped him, driving him to the ground. He had his knife out and without thinking slit the man's throat.

He was shocked by how easy it was to take the life of another person. He was unnerved watching the man's eyes go blank as the blood flow from the wound slowed to a trickle. The words from the captain helped a little.

He was still numb from his actions as they headed towards the extraction zone. He allowed his training to take over and automatically followed his team efficiently to safety.

Back at the base they were debriefed. Justin met with a military psychologist as he worked through this latest phase of his training program.

It was the psychologist's task to determine if taking a human life affected the mental and emotional stability of the soldier. If they could not adjust to the fact this was an expected part of their job, they were quickly re-assigned to other duties.

In his assessment of the young lieutenant, the doctor reported him fit for duty. Justin's place in Special Ops secure.

He was granted a week's leave and spent most of it prowling the bars in town. After an evening downing beer and whiskey, he would either take a cab back to his quarters on the base or spend the night with some woman he picked up.

He went back to work and eventually justified his actions by telling himself he was working for the best interests of the country he served.

There was truth in the saying: "if you say the lie often enough and loud enough, you will come to believe it."

Icthus

Chapter Twenty-five

Jo shook her head as they received the news from the Provost of the university that Caleb had been chosen to give the student commencement address. "What is it about you that you always get chosen to give the commencement speech?"

Caleb grinned and shrugged. "I don't know. Maybe it is my dashing good looks and witty repartee."

"We've had this conversation before so my response is going to be the same."

She threw a pillow at him and returned to her own studies, as finals were coming up and they were preparing to leave this institution.

After he finished his studies at the Bible institute, he chose to pursue his love of computers and entered an engineering program. He had earned several scholarships to attend the prestigious educational institution and they were gracious enough to defer his entrance for a year.

Credits for his time at the institute were worth almost two years of classes at the university. He was able to take care of most of his general education requirements and in the following four years had been able to complete not only his undergraduate degree, but most of the requirements for his masters.

He did not have to worry about looking for a job after grad. Companies were feverishly courting him. He had several lucrative offers and prayerfully considered where God would like him to go.

It was not an easy decision and he spent several sessions fasting and praying. They had always planned to return to their beloved home and work with the Assembly there. However, there were other doors that appeared to be opening and they wanted to be absolutely sure of God's leading.

One thing was for sure, they would be returning home after graduation for something very important: their marriage.

Caleb and Jo had sat down with their parents when they went home for the spring break. They discussed the options. The couple would need to earn an income and computer scientists were in demand. Growth of the still relatively new technology industry was exploding exponentially.

Caleb also met with the Elders of North Woods. They were extremely interested for the young couple to return to their home church and work with them to further the ministry. They prayed with him and agreed to stand by any decision they made.

They returned to school for the last weeks of their studies. Jo had decided to go in to education and was completing her studies for a teaching degree. They sent out many resumés. They even had a few interviews. They were not totally surprised due to the lack of opportunities and offers from their home town.

As graduation drew nearer, recruiters presented Caleb with some very interesting and lucrative offers. Fortune 500 companies were willing to offer a great deal in terms of salaries and benefits in attempts to entice him to accept employment with them.

Caleb knew in order to support him-self and his soon to be wife, he needed to earn an income. It was also his desire to serve God in the place he grew up in and still loved. The two goals did not seem to be on the same path.

He reluctantly accepted a position with one of the companies. After they were married they would locate to a suburban community outside of Toronto where he would be working in one of the gleaming office towers in the downtown core.

He once again gave the commencement address to the graduating class. He smile and accepted the congratulations of his parents, the faculty who had educated him and the many friends they would soon be leaving.

They packed up their belongings and drove to the apartment where they would be living in a few weeks. As a signing bonus, the company which Caleb decided to work for had provided them with a living allowance which included the apartment.

They would be able to live there for a year. After that they could purchase it as a condominium or relocate to another location. The company was a multinational one and Caleb could transfer to any of their offices throughout the world.

Jo was offered a teaching position in the local high school and with The University of Toronto nearby, Caleb could work on finishing his masters and pursue a doctorate.

Caleb and Jo felt a peace about the decision they had made. They were confident they were led by God to where they decided to start their married life together. There was a vibrant Assembly there with a lot of young couples.

Caleb and Jo had already met with the Elders and they were looking forward to them settling into their community and family. The Elders at North Woods reluctantly gave their commendation. They were disappointed the couple would not be moving back home.

They were aware God had a different path for them to follow for now. They knew the couple would be back for regular visits as they were still a part of the family.

Caleb and Jo had time to leave their belongings at the apartment and then headed home to begin the next step of their great adventure.

Chapter Twenty-six

It was a perfect June afternoon: sunny and warm but not hot. A slight breeze rustled the leaves of the majestic oaks. They were standing on the grounds of North Woods Chapel. In a few minutes, Jo would come from the farmhouse and walk up the aisle made by a roll of white material.

A string quartet played quietly as Caleb moved into position on the arbor under the trees. Doc, smiling broadly was facing the audience. Duncan was standing beside Caleb, serving as the best man.

Caleb had wished it was Justin standing beside him. They had made tentative plans for him to do those duties. However Justin had been called out of the country on an assignment and it looked like he wouldn't make if back in time.

Knowing Justin's crazy work schedule, he asked Duncan if he would be available for the honors in the event Justin couldn't make it.

Caleb thought often of his childhood friend and prayed regularly for him. They occasionally received postcards from the places Justin had visited in his work. Caleb thought about the very different paths they had taken. He was starting his career and Justin had been at his for over five years. He was getting married and Justin didn't pursue long-term relationships.

Doc motioned to the gathered guests to stand. Caleb turned around to see his bride coming toward him on the arm of her father. She was a vision in white.

He recalled her with pigtails bouncing down her back as she raced him up the tree of the fort or challenged him to a bike duel. They had grown up together and had become best friends.

Now they were going to be formally joined together as husband and wife.

People tended to be a little skeptical when they said they were childhood sweethearts. They had known that they were meant to be together. She smiled at him as she came closer to him. She decided not to wear a veil and her hair was woven with miniature roses and baby's breath.

Jo and her father stopped in front of him and Doc began the ceremony. "Who gives this woman to this man?"

Mr. Collins winked at Caleb. "Her mother and I do."

He kissed her on the cheek and put her hand in Caleb's. He then turned and sat down beside his wife, who was smiling, a damp hanky crumpled in her hand attempting to hold back her tears of joy.

Doc smiled and opened his Bible. He Began "Dearly beloved, we are gathered here to witness the marriage of Caleb Martin Jones to Joanne Darlene Collins. We understand marriage is a sacred and honorable institution created by God. Man and woman together. We read in Genesis two: *'And the LORD God said, 'It is not good that man should be alone; I will make him a helper comparable to him.*

'Out of the ground the LORD God formed every beast of the field and every bird of the air, and brought them to Adam to see what he would call them. And whatever Adam called each living creature, that was its name.

'So Adam gave names to all cattle, to the birds of the air, and to every beast of the field. But for Adam there was not found a helper comparable to him.

'And the LORD God caused a deep sleep to fall on Adam, and he slept; and He took one of his ribs, and closed up the flesh in

its place. Then the rib which the LORD *God had taken from man He made into a woman, and He brought her to the man.*

'And Adam said: "This is now bone of my bones and flesh of my flesh; She shall be called Woman, because she was taken out of Man."

'Therefore a man shall leave his father and mother and be joined to his wife, and they shall become one flesh.'

"There is a saying that God did not create Eve from Adam's foot to be put under him, nor from his head to be over him, but from his side, near his heart, to be loved and protected by him.

"Although I've known this couple from when they were children, and when Jo's parents despaired her ever becoming a young lady, these two became good friends. This friendship survived the teen years and even into the college years and blossomed into more than a friendship.

"They have chosen to commit themselves to each other as husband and wife. This covenant relationship they undertake is a picture of the relationship Christ has described with us; that of the bride and bridegroom.

"Each one has agreed to specific responsibilities in this agreement. We are here to witness their declaration of commitment to one another today."

He turned and addressed Caleb. "Caleb, please repeat after me."

They signed the license and walked back up the aisle as husband and wife. Their attendants followed them and then their parents. They stood in a line under the trees as their guests filed by and offered their congratulations.

They stood and smiled, and sat and smiled and stood and smiled some more as the photographer took pictures for them. There was also a friend who was videotaping.

The reception followed for their guests. They had set up small open-air tents around the chapel grounds with tables and chairs for people to sip ice tea and nibble on sandwiches and other finger foods. Caleb and Jo walked from table to table, stopping to visit and chat with their guests.

Jo spotted him first. Justin, in his dress uniform was walking up the driveway toward the festivities. She turned and tugged on Caleb's arm and pointed. He turned and a big grin broke out as he recognized his childhood buddy. He whistled, turned and excused himself, grabbed Jo's arm and headed towards Justin.

Justin grinned and embraced the two of them. This was their first reunion since they graduated from high school six years before. He stood back and looked at them. "Well it's about time. I thought you would have had her knocked up and married six months after grad."

Jo punched him on the arm. "You are totally so crude, Jones. Haven't changed a bit."

Justin smiled and kissed her on the cheek. "Yeah, it's good to see you too. Sorry I wasn't here for the actual ceremony. I got back into the country last night couldn't get a flight out until this morning."

He grinned over at Caleb. "I'm sorry I couldn't get here in time to stand with you buddy."

Caleb was also grinning. "Well, at least you're here. The three musketeers back together, if only for a few hours."

He stood back and looked at his friend. "You look a bit too fancy for a Grunt. What are you now? A General or something"

"I wish! Only a lieutenant."

"Have you had a chance to see your mom yet?" asked Jo as she linked one arm with his and the other with Caleb.

"No. I literally got off the plane, grabbed a rental and drove straight here."

"Well this is a special wedding gift." said Jo. "And a surprise for your mother, who is here somewhere."

They continued back toward the reception. They were almost back to the tables when Mrs. Jones caught sight of Justin and let out a scream of delight. She rushed over to the trio and wrapper her arms around her son. He gave her a big hug and swung her around. "Surprise!"

She stood back and looked at him, tears streaming down her face. "I can't believe your here. Show up for a friend's wedding but can't make it to visit your old mother a couple of times a year."

Justin laughed. "Mom. I was here at Christmas. It's not like I can come home every weekend you know."

They sat down at a table and the couple left mother and son to visit and catch up on their news. Caleb and Jo continued to circulate among their guests. There would be time to visit later.

Icthus

Chapter Twenty-seven

Justin joined the couple for the family dinner held after the reception had wound down. He didn't want to intrude, but Caleb and Jo insisted that he come with them. They had prepared for the possibility of him being there to share their day and had included him in the head count for the private celebration at the hotel.

After the meal ended, he joined the small group as they waved the couple off as they left for their hotel suite. He drove to his mother's place and brought in the small bag he had thrown together before heading to the airport.

The light was still good and he decided to go for a drive to check out some of the old haunts. He drove up Robertson Lake Road and parked at the small lot which was the head of the trail leading to The Bluffs overlooking the valley. It was a warm spring evening. The sun cast long shadows from the edge of the cliff. A few peregrine falcons soared on the warm air currents.

He sat down on a rough-hewn log bench and stared at the blackened fire pit. He had fond memories of this place, from hanging out with his high school chums, spending nights up here camping out with Caleb and sometimes Jo. It was the place he first smoked a joint with some other friends; the place where he lost his virginity. He was surprised at the depth of nostalgia he was experiencing.

Sometimes he wished he could share with Caleb and Jo the real nature of his work with the military. He had kept enough secrets from them while they were together.

He pulled out a pack of cigarettes from his pocket and flipped one into his mouth. He lit it and took a deep drag on it, blowing the smoke into the air.

He sighed. He did not regret his choice, but as his commanding officer indicated, the career path he had chosen was a lonely one. Only his immediate co-workers knew what he really did. Then it depended on the level of security clearance a person had to know the exact extent of his activities.

He was not that surprised Jo and Caleb were still together. It was a pretty obvious call even before they graduated from high school. Nor did it surprise him that they had not become lovers before tonight. He remembered their faith was very important to them. From the time Caleb had made his profession of faith he was interested in doing it right.

He threw the cigarette on the ground and stepped on it, twisting his foot to make sure it was out. He didn't have much of a chance to spend with the happy couple today. Well, he wasn't really expecting they would jump on their bikes and take off for the Grotto or the fort and hang out.

He had to admit to himself he was a little envious of his friends. They had a special relationship. He was lucky if his relationships lasted three months. It was not a good idea to get into any major commitment with another person when you never knew when or where you were going; or if you would ever come back. It wasn't fair to a partner to have to live with such uncertainty.

He already knew from coworkers the divorce rate for agents was probably eighty per cent; closer to one hundred per cent. He quickly found out keeping secrets takes a toll.

He stood up reached into his shirt pocket and pulled out another cigarette. He lit it and inhaled deeply. Justin walked to the edge of the cliff, ignoring the danger sign and looked down.

He could see small trees clinging tenaciously to the rock face. At the bottom a field of sharp stones chipped off over thousands of years of weather exposure covered the ground like a textured quilt. He looked up at the coasting falcons and stretched out his arms in imitation. There were times when he wished he could just fly free like them.

Justin wasn't sure how long he stood there, arms outstretched, eyes closed. He felt the cool evening breeze and opened his eyes again. The sun was starting to set and the shadows were growing longer.

He turned and headed back to the trail. Although he was use to navigating at night on his missions, he wasn't at work here and wasn't interested in attempting to negotiate the steep path in the dark.

Icthus

Icthus

Chapter Twenty-eight

Jo curled up against Caleb her head on his shoulder. He had his arm around her. She rubbed her hand on his chest. "This is weird."

"What? The chest hair? You have seen me before without a shirt on. Of course, now I get to see you without your shirt on. I'm glad you don't have any chest hair; it would have been a little awkward."

She gave him a playful slap. "That's not what I meant. I mean it's different. We're no longer just friends, we're soul mates, lovers. I know that by today's standards we could have justified the physical relationship before we actually got married. But this is special. I'm glad we waited."

He nodded. "Me, too. Although there were times I didn't think I had the will power. You are one hot chick! I think many people thought we were already sleeping together and pretending we weren't."

"No matter how tempting it got to give in to the physical, it was important to me to honor God and to honor you by waiting for the right time. This time."

She inhaled his fragrance and let out her breath in a long slow sigh. "Yeah, I actually had some of my friends ask how long I had been hooked up with you and if you were great in bed."

He turned his head sideways and gave her a "well tell the rest of it" look. "Really? What did you tell them?"

She giggled. "I told them when we actually 'did it' I would tell them."

He chuckled. "And what are you going to tell them?"

135

She licked her finger and put it to his chest making a sizzling sound. "Hot, hot, hot!"

He laughed and rolled her into his arms. "What time are your parent's expecting us for the gift opening?

She gave him a sly smile. "When we get there. We are newlyweds after all."

The couple made their appearance at the Collins' late afternoon. Jo had been right in their expectations. The Whites were also there sitting on the patio, chatting and sipping ice tea. Mrs. Jones and Justin arrived shortly after they did. Other people were also starting to arrive, carrying platters and bowls of food. It looked like they were having a potluck picnic.

Caleb had a chance to look around and noticed there were several portable tables set up from the chapel. One was piled high with brightly wrapped gifts. At one end was a wishing well where people had dropped in cards yesterday during the reception.

Along the north side of the patio four barbeques were set up. He noticed John and Terry from the chapel going over to them and turning them on. He guessed they were the grill masters for the day. Another table set up nearby was quickly being loaded down with the food the guests were bringing.

He walked over to his parents who stood up and gave him a big hug. His mother planted a kiss on his cheek. "We weren't expecting this crowd, Mom. I thought this was just family and a few friends."

She laughed. "Caleb, honey, these are family and friends. They watched you and Jo grow up and are a part of your lives. Besides, you know North Woods, any excuse for fellowship."

Mr. White grinned. "It's a good thing there is so much food. You two will have to replenish your strength!"

"Dad!"

Jo came over and gave her new parents hugs and kisses on the cheek. "Wow! It's going to take a while to get used to thinking of you as Mom and Dad. But then I almost lived at your house anyway and now it's official. I can raid the fridge before Caleb gets there!"

Mr. and Mrs. White laughed. "Honey, you can come and raid my fridge anytime you want," replied her new mother-in-law. "I'll even make sure you have a Taser ready to keep my son at bay."

"Caleb feigned an injured look, "Now the truth comes out. She was always your favorite!"

She reached up and squeezed his cheek. "That's right, Muffin. And it only took you twenty-seven years to officially make her a part of the family."

She turned and put her arm around Jo. "Ok, Daughter-in-love. Let's get to the food before these bottomless pits eat it all. Are any of you guys going to say grace so we can chow down?"

Grace was said and people gestured to the couple of honor to move towards the food-laden table. They picked up their plates and cutlery and worked their way along buffet, loading their plates down with potato and macaroni salads, coleslaw, barbequed hamburgers and sausages, and other summer picnic standards.

Caleb and Jo walked over to one of the tables set up for people to eat at. Justin walked over to them with his plate, placed it on the table and sat down with them. He grinned as he picked up his fork and dug into the potato salad. "Not quite like old times, but it sure is good to be here with you. So besides this, what else has been going on in your lives?"

They laughed and shared the highlights from the last time they were together. Well, almost everything. Justin wove his cover story about his administrative duties and the places he had been posted on the various Canadian military bases and embassies around the world.

"Good party." He commented. "The only thing missing is the beer."

Caleb shook his head and pretended mock surprise. "What, you don't have a secret stash in the trunk of your car?"

"Nah, that's so high school."

They wished they could have spent more time together. Justin was only up for the day and had booked a seat on the last flight out. He watched as Caleb and Jo opened their gifts and enjoyed the afternoon with them. God only knew how long it would be before they had the opportunity to be together again.

Chapter - Twenty-nine

The man struggled against the pressure holding his head under the water. Pain shot through his skull as he was jerked up and gasped for air. His head was forced under again. Finally, the waterboarding ceased. The subject sat in his chair, gasping deeply.

Justin moved to give the man a chance to look at his examiner: His face mottled with bruises ...eyes half-closed. "So, where is the location of your headquarters? I don't know about you, but I can keep this up indefinitely. How long this take is entirely up to you."

He pulled the terrorist up by his shirt and positioned him so he could stare in the man's half-closed eyes. "No one knows you are here. Your answers will determine how long you will get to live."

He dropped the man and watched hi flop back into the chair, panting. He glared at his tormentor. "Death to you, infidel." and spat at Justin's feet.

Justin raised an eyebrow and casually walked over to him. His backhand knocked the other man off the chair and onto the floor. Justin kicked him in the abdomen and then groin. He smiled coldly as his subject cried out. "No, it's death to you and your cause."

He walked back to toward the door, opened it and motioned to the guard. "Put that piece of crap back into the hole."

He kept walking, not bothering to look back to see if his orders were being followed. He knew they were.

The outside of the building was a non-descript warehouse. It was not much different than the hundred or so warehouses and other offices in the industrial park. But inside was a hive of activity. This base was not listed on the roster of military bases. Most of the Canadian armed forces personnel were unaware of the existence of this installation. This was a part of the network of the covert world of Black Ops and counter terrorism.

He walked into his office and glanced up the monitor. He watched the guards dragged the prisoner down the hall to the detention cell. The cell was four feet by six with a tap for water and a hole in the ground for a toilet. The only light in the cubicle was from a small rectangular window high on the door. The detention cells were sound proof and climate controlled. They could bake their prisoners or freeze them to obtain the desired results.

It was his third visit to this particular base. He moved from one assignment to the next, always preparing for the next mission, executing it or debriefing. He quickly learned these places were anonymous, non-descript. Secrecy was the norm and there was no such thing as normalcy.

He picked up the remote and turned the monitor off. He sat at his desk and pulled out the keyboard. Typing in his code and waited for the system to acknowledge his identity. The monitor blinked access granted. The video feed automatically launched.

"Colonel, how are you?"

"Very well Justin. How is the interrogation proceeding? Do we have any viable intel yet?"

"No sir. He is one tough nut. But I will crack him. We have not attempted chemical interrogation yet. It doesn't leave much left of their mental capacities by the time we gather the information we require."

"Copy that. We are under a time constraint. Previous intel suggests the target has started to implement the first stages of his plan."

Justin replied. "Copy that. What is our time frame?"

"Seventy-two hours."

He kept a blank face. "That doesn't give us much time. This is the closest we've been to locating their leader in two years. If we can shut him down, we may be able to neutralize the organization."

Colonel Smith nodded. "Well done, Justin. You are authorized to use lethal force to obtain the intelligence we need to launch this mission. Report in thirty-six hours: mark."

"Mark."

The video feed ended. Justin allowed himself to relax. One way or another, the prisoner would divulge the required information. He would have the location of the target.

He picked up the phone and dialed an internal number. "Doctor Brown? How are you today? That's great. Can you report to my office in fifteen minutes? We have something to discuss."

Four days later, Justin rendezvoused with the Colonel and the rest of his team. They had obtained the information they were seeking. Further reconnaissance spoke to the veracity of that information.

They successfully infiltrated the target's secret base. No one escaped.

After the debriefing session Justin stood at the sink in his office lavatory. He splashed cold water on his face. He looked at the person in the mirror and wondered if there was any humanity left in him at all.

The first person he killed had caused him to be physically ill. Ten years later he could calmly snap his opponent's neck and continue on with his mission without a second thought: weapon cocked and ready to use if detected

He lost track of the people deemed threats to Canada's sovereignty that he had neutralized indirectly or directly. He, like his team, preferred to use that word. It was better than to call it what it was: murder. They justified it by telling themselves they were fighting a secret war that allowed their fellow countrymen to still keep the illusion they were sleeping safe in their beds.

He reached for a towel and dried himself off. He took one last look at the person in the mirror before he turned and walked out of the room his hand automatically brushing the light switch as he exited.

Chapter Thirty

Caleb and Jo finished up their weekly group study. They were studying biblical prophecy: a topic that held fascination for many, but also many who misunderstood the subject.

Caleb led the group and had explained that when the Bible was written, over twenty-five per cent of it was prophetic in nature. The fulfillment of prophecy to date had been perfect.

They sat around the table with their notebooks open looking expectantly at Caleb.

"John, would you look up Isaiah forty-four, verses six through eight please."

They all turned in their Bibles to the requested passage and John started to read. *"Thus says the LORD, the King of Israel, and his Redeemer, the LORD of hosts: 'I am the First and I am the Last; Besides Me there is no God.*

And who can proclaim as I do? Then let him declare it and set it in order for Me,

Since I appointed the ancient people. and the things that are coming and shall come,

"Let them show these to them. Do not fear, nor be afraid; Have I not told you from that time, and declared it?You are My witnesses. Is there a God besides Me?

"Indeed there is no other Rock; I know not one.' "

They looked expectantly at Caleb. "OK. What does the passage say about the purpose of prophecy?"

Cathy, one of the other participants spoke up. "Well it seems to be a declaration that He is the only God and prophecy is His way of proving it. Only an omniscient being would have knowledge of future events."

"Excellent." said Caleb. "If we all did our homework this last week, we should have come up with a few other reasons as well."

He looked expectantly around the table. Jo smiled. Caleb was not one to provide the answers for people who were fully capable of finding them for themselves.

Carol spoke up. "Isaiah forty-two verses twenty-two to twenty-four indicated that as well. There was another verse in Isaiah." she consulted her notebook. "Here it is; forty-eight: five. *Before it came to pass I proclaimed it to you. Lest you should say, "My idol has done them, and my carved image and my molded image have commanded them."*

"Good work, Carol," commented Caleb. "Jesus gave His disciples a similar answer about His prophetic utterances. John thirteen verse nineteen says: *'Now I tell you before it comes, that when it does come to pass, you may believe that I am He.'*"

Jo spoke up. "I discovered prophecy was also used to indicate God's will. Samuel prophesied to Saul about the day's events to prove that God was taking the kingdom away from him."

Caleb nodded. "It was also a test of faith. Joseph instructed the children of Israel to take his bones back to the Promised Land."

Sam looked over the group. "But how does this tie in with today?"

Caleb looked over at him. "Well. Daniel was told that his prophecies would be locked up until the time of the end *when many shall run to and fro, and knowledge shall increase.*

"Many have wondered and struggled over that phrasing until recently when it suggested this is referring to our times. People are running to and fro. We have the ability to fly all over the world. We communicate faster than light. The twentieth and twenty-first centuries have seen knowledge increase at an exponential rate.

Caleb took a sip of his tea and set the cup back on the table. "I work in an industry that twenty-years ago did not exist. You know the first computer our school board owned was four times the size of this room. Now you can buy a pocket calculator at the local dollar store that has more computing power."

They all nodded. They used computers on a daily basis. "We are becoming more and more dependent upon these devices for our daily living. Because of them, our world is changing and becoming more like a community than separate nations."

"Did you find anything else about the purpose for prophecy?" Caleb asked, continuing to go through the material.

They worked their way through this lesson. "Ok. Are there any questions about what we discussed tonight? Going... going... gone!"

Everybody indicated they were good. "Ok, next week we are going to take a look at how to study predictive literature and maybe even start to look at the major themes of biblical prophecy. Thank-you for coming and thanks to our hosts for having us. Next week we are meeting at our place. God bless and see you Sunday."

They filed out of the house with the other study members and got in the car to go home. Jo placed her seat back and lay with her eyes closed. Caleb glanced over at her. They had been married five years and she was more beautiful and lovelier than the day they were united in marriage. He could make out a furrow across her brow. "Headache again?"

"Mmmm. Yes. I think I'm going overdoing it. Probably need to get my eyes checked and get a new prescription for my glasses." She looked over at him and smiled. "You did a wonderful job tonight. Your teaching gifts get better with time. But then, so do you."

He grinned. "I was just thinking the same of you."

She turned her head to stare out of the window at the passing street lights. "I was thinking..."she trailed off.

"What about dear?

"We've been married what, five years now."

"More or less."

"Well, as it's September, I would say slightly more," she returned.

"Ok. So we've been married a few months longer. To me it seems just like yesterday when you, Justin and me were flying through mud puddles feet off the handle bars and water spraying everywhere."

"Is that how you still see me? Eight years old in pigtails and braces?"

"Not always. There is racing to be the first to the top of the fort, you trying to tie that ribbon on the goat's tail at Vacation Bible School, you standing in your prom dress. I knew then that you would be my wife."

She smiled back at him, "That sure of yourself, huh?"

"Yup! Anyway, let's go back to 'I was thinking...'"

"I think it's time to start a family."

Caleb was so surprised by this statement he almost lost control of the car as he turned to stare are her. "Really?"

"Well, you know our parents have been hinting about how nice it would be to have a grandbaby or two to spoil. Besides, after five years, I think we've proven that we didn't sleep together before we were married. We did decided to wait until we had been married a while and gained some stability."

"Well we can start tonight if you like?"

She laughed. "You have to catch me first! I can still climb trees faster than you. And I'm smaller too!"

He put a little lead into his foot. "Lucky for me we live in an apartment. I have longer legs and can take the stairs two at time!"

Icthus

Chapter Thirty-one

Caleb was in the middle of a video conference with several of his coworkers from their various offices around the globe. "Hey, Joe," he said to his Australian counterpart. "What's the weather going to be like tomorrow?"

"It's beautiful here for a fine spring morning, mate." came the answer with an accompanying chuckle at the old joke.

He noticed the New York feed just coming on line. "Hey Smith, it's eight-thirty. Line at Starbucks pretty long, eh?"

John Smith grimaced as he sipped the coffee. "It's no Timmie's, but it'll do in a pinch."

Caleb noticed that all the parties were now on line. "Great, let's get started. Now did each of you get the meeting package which I e-mailed to everyone? "

The participants all indicated they had received the packet and had gone over the contents. "Ok. It appears we are on target for the release of our new software package. My team here is reasonably sure the bugs have been worked out which Research and Development identified. We are also getting a lot of positive feedback from the beta testers. Does anyone have anything else to add?"

Caleb paused for the other participants. Joe spoke, "Our R and D here are ready to give the final product a nod. How about you John?"

"Well our guys do have a couple of questions on a couple of code lines, but they are happy with the results so far and our beta testers are mostly positive. I thin..."

He looked startled as they could hear an explosion coming over the speakers. "What the he.." The feed from New York disappeared.

Caleb picked up the phone and attempted to contact John while sending out the request for the video conference. The phone was dead. He tried John's cell phone. The line gave back a busy signal.

Jen, Caleb's assistant, walked into the conference room pale and shaking. "Oh, my God! A plane just crashed into the World Trade Center!"

Shock held Caleb and the other participants speechless. Caleb reached for the remote for the television. "Which one?"

Jen was sobbing. "One."

Caleb closed his eyes. That's were there New York office was. John was in that tower. He turned back to his computer console. "Did you guys get that? A plane crashed into the World Trade Center."

They nodded. "Let's suspend this meeting. I need to ascertain the extant of the damage and if our team there is ok."

They quickly logged off. The phone started to ring. He looked at the number and saw that it was Dave, his boss. "Hey, Dave. Yes... I know. We were in the middle of our vid-con when it happened. I can't get a hold of him or the office, hard line nor any cell. "

He continued to look at the carnage on the television monitor. Smoke was pouring from the gaping wound in the side of the building. "Do you know what floors were hit?" he asked.

"Not yet, Cal. I will keep attempting to contact someone. Meanwhile, shut it down for the day. There are more important things at the moment."

Although he informed the staff they were free to go home they were reluctant to leave. They all knew John and were still staring at the screen with a sense of denial still fighting in their minds as the destruction unfolded on the screen.

Caleb picked up his cell and called his wife. "Oh, honey. This is just terrible. And you haven't been able to contact John at all?"

"No. I can't tell from the news feed where the planes hit. It looks near the floors where our offices are."

He was talking to her and watching the television when the second tower erupted into flames. "Jo! Another plane just crashed into the... the other tower!"

He stared horrified by the scenes of destruction. "This is not an accident, Jo. It is a declaration of war. We just don't know with whom yet. Look, I'm going to stay here for a while and see what I can do from my end to locate our team in New York. Dave is working at it too."

"Ok. I am at work, but I think we are going to send the kids home early. If that's the case I'll come over there and be with you. Oh, Caleb, we will need to pray."

He ended the call and sat with the rest of the staff watching the people streaming out of the towers, hoping for a glimpse of any of their co-workers. Caleb had been there on business on several occasions over his tenure with the company.

He had been offered the chance to run the New York office, but had turned it down. He felt the Lord did not want him to go. So it was John who had been tapped for the position.

The commentator broke in with the announcement there were reports of another plane crashing into the Pentagon. Caleb shook his head. It was war indeed. A few minutes later came the report of yet a fourth plane crashing into the ground in Pennsylvania.

Ten minutes later came the announcement the United State had closed its air space and instructed all planes to land. They would not allow any aircraft to enter their borders.

They watched the screen as people started screaming and running from the towers. They could see one tower start to collapse and disappear into a cloud of dust and debris. Caleb groaned. This was getting worse by the second. The cameraman also started to run for cover as the hungry cloud reached out engulfing everything in its path.

He looked up as another person came into the office. He smiled when he recognized his wife. Caleb quickly stood up and went over to her, giving her a big hug. "One of the towers collapsed."

She nodded. "Any word yet on John or the staff?"

He shook his head. Jo could see he was exerting tremendous control over his emotions right now. He was carrying a facade of calmness. John and Caleb were not only coworkers and good friends. They were members of the same Assembly. John and his wife were regular members of their Bible study group as well. They were more that colleagues, they were family members. He had tried to contact Trish when he couldn't reach John and had no success. "Caleb, did you activate the prayer chain?"

"No. will you do that for me?"

Jo nodded and pulled her cellphone out of her purse. She dialed the coordinator's number and waiting for a few seconds. Quickly she explained that John was in the tower when the plane hit and haven't been able to establish contact with them. She returned her attention to the television with everyone else in the room. She reached out and took hold of Caleb's hand. It was cold. So was hers.

She gasped in horror as she watched the second tower collapse in a mushroom cloud of dust and debris. "There must have been thousands of people in those building. Oh, Caleb what pain their families must be suffering."

He looked over to her and saw the tears coursing down her cheeks. Gently touching her face, Caleb knew his own face was wet with tears. He knew the world would never be the same again.

Icthus

Chapter Thirty-two

Justin was already at his office when they were placed on full alert. News of the attacks in New York and Washington D.C. triggered the U.S. military to declare a DEFCON THREE. The Canadian Joint Chiefs also declared a state of emergency. They quickly mobilized the military airports as well as any available airport able to handle all incoming flights which had been diverted.

Justin's team reported for duty. They were monitoring their sources for information as to the nature of the attacks and looking for any clues about the perpetrators. Another team was sifting through reports, gleaning pertinent data to work on completing the puzzle. Justin was talking with his counterparts in the other bases, sending each other updates over the secure channels.

He already knew the Prime Minister and his cabinet, as well as the opposition leaders were being relocated to a secure location in case these attacks spread to Canada.

Richards nodded to him and handed him a piece of paper. He turned to his monitor and caught the attention of Colonel Smith. "Major, I think we have a lead on the perpetrators. I am faxing you the information now."

"Copy that."

A few minutes later, the man was handed a paper and began to look over it. He looked up at the camera. "Justin, how accurate is this?"

"I got a look at it about two minutes before I contacted you. We had discussed Al Qadai several months ago as a possible threat to us. We were getting unsubstantiated rumors about this group planning an attack, but could not verify any details with accuracy.

"We do know there were several people we have been monitoring with ties to this and other extremist groups for several months. Our intel suggests that within the last two weeks, most of them had entered the U.S."

Colonel Smith nodded. "Too bad our U.S. counterparts aren't more willing to share information and work together. I bet they are going to lock down the country tight. Ok. Keep monitoring and send me updates every hour. If something major develops contact me immediately."

"Copy that, Major."

Justin broke off contact, bent his head over his desk and started reading the reports which were starting to pile up on his desk. He glanced over at his coffee pot. Good. It was full. The next few days were going to be long and intense.

In the days following 9/11 as it began to be called, Justin and his team were able to determine the attacks had been aimed at the United States. There were no determining factors to indicate Canada was ever a target.

The incident not only affected the reorganization of security measures in the Unites States, but throughout the western world. Justin's organization was given more power to secure the borders of their own country.

Laws were being passed which, while aimed at terrorists, the wording was broad enough in describing threats against the Sovereignty of the nation to mean whatever the government wanted it to mean.

Other caveats and laws passed quietly in following years eroded away the rights Canadians had always considered inalienable.

The Joint Task Force received authorization to construct detainment centers. That was not difficult to accomplish. As nearly eighty per cent of the population lived within 400 kilometers of their southern neighbor, there was lots of room to build these facilities without the knowledge or consent of the majority of citizens.

The Canadian government was preparing for war: The war against its own citizens.

Icthus

Chapter Thirty-one

Caleb finished reading the article about alleged concentration camps being built in the United States. He put the paper down and looked around the study group. Six months had gone by since that horrific morning when over 3,000 people became instant victims in a war they did not know they were fighting. "The events that we are experiencing are just the tip of the iceberg. And we know from science that ninety per cent of the berg is hidden underwater."

He was looking for discussion material for the small group he and Jo were leading. There were a lot of claims, charges and theories in cyberspace; the conspiracy claims had grown substantially with much conjecture and very little hard evidence to back most up.

There group was examining biblical prophecy. Many in the group were very interested in how the current events could be interpreted in light of what the Bible had to say about future events.

"We can speculate about how these events correlate to the Bible, but we need to avoid the danger of becoming dogmatic about it. We could ask ourselves why would the U.S. need to build detainment centers capable of holding thousands of its own citizens? We should ask ourselves if our government is planning the same thing. After all, we detained not only Japanese immigrants, but also Italian and German ones as well. That piece of information is not often shared with the general public."

I personally think our rights are being slowly taken away from us. I heard a story about an experiment how if a frog was placed in hot water, it would immediately jump out. If the frog was put in cold water and the temperature was slowly raised, then the frog would acclimatize to the rising temperature until it was boiled."

If we do not realize that our rights are slowly being taken away, we won't notice until it is too late. But enough of conspiracy theories: let's get back on track here."

He grinned at the group. "Now if the person who keeps bringing up conspiracy theories would kindly refrain…" he paused as they broke out laughing, "Oh, wait… that's me."

They continued their study. Jo did not accompany him that night. Her headaches had been becoming more severe. There were times when she did not gain any relief. She had her appointment with the optometrist and discovered nothing wrong with her eyes.

She had gone to her general practitioner who had run a battery of tests and had found nothing out of the ordinary. After they discovered the medication for the headaches was losing its effectiveness, he recommended she see a neurologist.

The appointment was next week. Caleb was concerned, but knew he could leave it in God's capable hands.

Icthus

Chapter Thirty-two

Jo leaned against the cool metal of her locker in the teacher's
lounge. It felt nice to her pounding head. The day had started
out great. Her almost constant migraines had abated and she
felt she could go to work that day.

Just after lunch she could feel the familiar buzz in the back of
her neck which signaled the start of another session. She had a
free period coming up and headed for her locker to get her
medication. Pills in hand she walked over to the water cooler to
get a glass of water.

Cynthia, a co-worker, was seated at the table marking tests. She
looked up in time to see Jo collapse on the floor and go into
convulsions. Jo could hear Cynthia's gasp and calling for help
before fading from consciousness.

Caleb arrived at the hospital shortly after Jo did. He went to the
emergency desk and the receptionist looked inquiringly at him.
"My wife Joanne White was just brought in by ambulance."

She looked at her computer terminal. "Ah, yes, Mr. White. She
is being examined by the ER doctor right now. Please have a
seat in the waiting room and someone will come to meet you."

He went to the designated room, but he was too tense to sit
down. He paced back and forth, mentally kicking himself for not
making her see a doctor sooner over these bloody headaches.
He looked up and whispered, "God, keep us in your hands."

Almost an hour passed before the nurse came to get him and
lead him to the room were Jo was. Lying on the gurney amidst
an array of machinery emitting soft beeps, she looked pale and
drawn.

He immediately hurried to her side and picked up her hand. Feeling his presence, she opened her eyes and smiled at him. She had a bruise on the side of her face where she had struck the floor when she fell.

The nurse notified the doctor of Caleb's presence. She indicated he would join them in the triage room in a few minutes. "Mr. White, is this the first time your wife has had a seizure like this?"

Caleb nodded. "Yes. This has never happened before."

Jo looked at both of them. "I told you that. I am not deaf you know. I'm lying right here."

Both the Doctor and Caleb smiled. "Do you know how long these headaches have been going on?"

Jo and Caleb looked at each other. "They probably started last summer. We thought her eyes had changed and were causing the them."

Caleb noticed the doctor's name tag read Lucas and smiled. "The optometrist indicated everything was ok, we then turned to the General Practitioner for further investigation. He had ordered a battery of tests and referred us to a neurologist when he could not find anything out of the ordinary. We were to meet with her later this week."

Dr. Lucas nodded and scribbled some notes on the clipboard that had been attached to the gurney. He looked at the monitors and then at Jo. "Have you had or noticed any bouts of sudden weakness or numbness on your right or left side?"

She shook her head negatively. "How about experiencing the loss of speech, blurring in your vision, or moments where you lost focus and couldn't remember where you were or what you were doing?"

"No, I don't recall any of that."

Caleb nodded his head. "Other than these headaches, there has been nothing else that accompanied them until today."

"What is the name of the neurologist you were going to see?"

"Dr. Phroneo."

Dr. Lucas continued to write on the clipboard. "She is one of the best in her field." He finished his writing and looked up at them again. "Ok, we are waiting for the standard blood work to come back from the lab. In the meantime, I have scheduled Mrs. White for an MRI and will contact Dr. Phroneo and let her know that you are here.

"Mr. White, you can wait with your wife and go with her to the diagnostics wing. There is a comfortable waiting room while she is in having the MRI done."

Caleb nodded and the doctor left them alone. He looked down at her, reached out with his other hand and gently brushed the hair from her face. He leaned over and gently touched her lips with his. "Caleb," she whispered. "I'm scared."

He smiled slightly and squeezed her hand. "So am I." he whispered in her ear.

He placed his hand on her forehead and closed his eyes. "Father of the universe; we come before you frightened and unsure. We come boldly before your throne to find the mercy we so desperately need. I pray for you to provide the doctors with wisdom and we are able to discover what the problem is. We continue to pray for understanding and healing. In Jesus name, we pray, Amen."

They could hear someone clearing their throat behind them and looked over. It was the nurse and another hospital worker. She saw that they were finished praying and smiled as she walked over to them. "They are ready for you."

She quickly turned off the monitors and disconnected the wires from Jo's head and chest. "The MRI works on magnet pulses." the nurse explained. "So we have to remove any metal because it would become attracted to the magnets and give a false image. That means we also have to remove all your jewelry for the procedure."

Jo reluctantly took off her wedding band. This was the first time she had removed it since Caleb put it on her finger nearly six years before. She pressed it into Caleb's hands. "Don't lose it, I want it back."

He smiled and removed the chain that was around his neck, undid the clasp, threaded the ring and put it back on. "It is right next to my heart, where you are."

He held her hand as they wheeled the gurney to the nuclear medicine department where the MRI machine was located. It was cold and she was shaking. They stopped at the desk to give the receptionist the paper work then wheeled her down the hall and around the corner. Caleb watched them until they turned the corner at the end of the hall.

He went to the nearby waiting room and seated himself on one of the brown leather chairs. The television was tuned to a local news program. He picked up one of the news magazines on the table. It was dated from three years ago: so much for current news.

He pulled out his cell phone. His fingers were shaking as he punched in the numbers. Eyes glistened from unshed tears. "Hey, Mom, Yeah I know I should be at work now. Something has happened and I need you to activate the prayer chain and go over to Jo's parents."

He explained what happened "I was going to call when we had some more definite answers before giving doing that, but I can't wait any longer."

"Oh, Son, you must be scared out of your mind. I will start our prayer chain and then head over to Alice and Bob's right away. Call when you have more news."

He felt better, but not by much. He punched in a second number to activate the prayer chain from the local Assembly. All there was left to do was wait and pray.

Icthus

Chapter Thirty-three

Brenda and Alice spent the next few hours sitting tensely and praying at the Collins household. Brenda had activated the prayer chain. Soon the chapel family would be aware of the crisis and would be in prayer.

She contacted her husband's office and left a message where to meet. Making sure the lights were off, she grabbed her purse and headed for the car.

Alice was at home when Brenda got there. One look at the woman's face and she knew something was wrong with her baby girl. Brenda enfolded the woman in a comforting embrace and both were crying. Their children were in pain and so were they.

Their husbands arrived over the next couple of hours. Alice prepared a light supper for the four of them which went largely untouched: every minute an eternity while they waited for news.

When Caleb finally called, they put him on the speaker so all of them could hear what he had to say. "Sorry this has taken so long. You know how hospitals are: hurry up and wait."

"How is Jo?" her mother asked.

"Resting comfortably, Mom C. They have given her a sedative to help her get some sleep."

They could hear the emotion in his voice. He was silent for a few moments while he got his thoughts together. "How are you, Son," his father asked.

"Not good."

More silence. "Umm... There is not an easy way to say this. Jo has a brain tumor. That is what has been causing her headaches."

They sat in stunned silence.

Caleb felt much the same way. He was still numb, a sense of unreality buzzed his brain. Dr. Phroneo came in an hour or so after the MRI had been completed. Jo had been transferred to a private hospital room. She and Caleb had been by themselves after the nurses had hooked up the monitors on her in case she had another seizure.

"Hi." said the pleasant dark-haired woman as she entered the room holding the binder which now held Jo's. "I guess I can cancel your appointment."

The doctor pulled up a tall stool beside the bed and sat down on it. "So, Jo; May I call you Jo?" She nodded.

She reached out a hand to Caleb and shook it. "And you are Caleb?"

"Yes."

The Doctor continued. "We tend to forget the spouse is involved in this just as much as the patient. I know you will have lots of questions in the next few weeks and months and we have a team here to help you."

Caleb looked at the physician. "Help us do what exactly?"

"The MRI has revealed your wife has a tumor located almost in the center of her brain. We are going to see if we can schedule a biopsy to confirm it, but in cases like this, ninety per cent of the time they are malignant. Often they are inoperable due to the location."

Caleb could feel his world slipping away from under him. He gripped the side of the bed to steady himself. He and Jo stared at each other, not sure what to say. She gripped his hand tighter.

Dr. Phroneo waited until she could see the couple was ready for her to continue. "I have called the oncologist to consult. We will know more after the biopsy has been completed. Because of the gravity of the situation, we are prepping the operating room now and a team will come in shortly to escort her there. We should know one way or the other within the next few hours."

Icthus

Chapter Thirty-four

Caleb relayed the diagnosis to their parents. "The surgical team is getting ready to take her up. They are going to do a biopsy and attempt to remove the tumor."

Alice and Brenda were holding each other, weeping freely. Caleb's father was fighting his emotions. Nothing he had taught his son would have prepared him for this. "Son, what hospital are you at?"

He told them. "Ok; we are going to arrange a flight there as soon as we can.."

"You don't need to do that, Dad."

"Yes we do, Son. It may be all of us or some of us. We will let you know as soon as we do."

Caleb didn't feel like arguing anymore. He was drained and empty. "Ok. Look I've got to go. The team is here and they are ready to take her to the operating room."

They quickly said their goodbyes.

Alice and Bob sat staring at each other for a few minutes before he spoke. "Ok. How are we going to do this? I can take an emergency leave and I've got some vacation time stocked up."

Alice stood up. "I am not staying here while my baby's life hangs in the balance."

He went over to her and put his arms around her. "I didn't suggest such a thing. Why don't you go pack a suitcase and I'll call the airport."

Brenda White picked up the phone and contacted the prayer chain with an update. When she had finished she also stood up with her husband and hugged Alice again. "It's in the Lord's hands." She gave a small laugh. "You know, I don't know how often I've said that to others in times of crisis, but I'm at peace knowing it's true.

She looked over to her husband and he nodded at her. "David, call the airline and see how quickly we can get down there."

She reached out and squeezed Alice and Bob's hands. "We are going to go home and get a suitcase together. We will call you as soon as we know what's going on."

It didn't take long to arrange for the flights and pack. Within the hour they were on their way to the airport.

Chapter Thirty-five

Caleb buried Jo a week after their sixth wedding anniversary. He stood at the graveside and stared at the polished oak coffin. A spray of roses and sunflowers graced the top.

They were standing in the small country cemetery in the community they had grown up in. Beside him were Jo's parents on one side of him and his parents on the other.

In his wildest nightmares, he never thought this day would come so soon. They were supposed to live until they were old and grey with their grandchildren and maybe great-grandchildren around them, if they were so blessed. He didn't even have a part of her in the child they planned to conceive.

She had been out of surgery and was sleeping when their parents arrived at the hospital. They were able to get seats on the same flight leaving later that evening. He looked up as they came into the room. The shock of the day's events had drained his reserves and he did nothing more than smile at them and turn back to gaze upon his beloved.

She lay on the bed, several intravenous bags with saline solutions and various drugs hung from a pole near her head. They collected into a single line which ran into her body. Monitors beeped and flashed vital signs in a monotonous pattern. Caleb had been there so long he tuned out the soft beeps they were making.

Jo had been in the operating room for several hours. Dr. Phroneo had come to sit with him in the lounge where he had been waiting for word. The grim expression on her face told Caleb what he needed to know. His shoulders shook in silent sobs.

The Doctor explained they were successful in obtaining a biopsy. They could not remove the entire tumor due to its location. She waited until the results confirmed the malignancy before coming to talk to him. She and the oncologist would meet with them tomorrow when Jo was more awake and go over possible treatment options.

Caleb gripped the coffee mug he had been holding so hard, he was surprised it didn't shatter in his hands. "How long are we talking here?"

Dr. Phroneo sighed. "I'm not one to speculate. Depending on your decisions over the next couple of days she could have weeks, or months. If the treatment is successful - years - maybe. This cancer is very aggressive. The oncologist will be able to better answer those questions. Your wife should be in her room within the next half hour."

She stood up to leave. She placed her hand on his shoulder. "I am truly sorry."

Caleb sat at the table for a long while, afraid that if he stood up his legs would no longer support him. He wondered where the strength would come from to carry on from this. He knew he had to dig deep into the well to support Jo. He wasn't sure he had a reservoir that deep.

He bowed his head and tried to pray. His heart and mind were frozen. He had no idea what to say: what to ask. He wanted his wife whole and healthy. He wanted the life they had planned together.

He walked over to the window and blindly stared out of it.

He was looking at a different path now, a fork in the road and for the first time in his life, he didn't know what to do.

Caleb turned slowly, walking carefully and deliberately as if the floor was made of glass and at any moment he would plunge though it. He wasn't sure how he made it back to the room. He pulled up the chair and sat down beside her once again.

She looked so pale. Her head swathed in bandages. He knew her long golden locks were in a garbage bag somewhere in the bio-waste disposal system. He picked up her hand and held it in his. She smiled slightly, as if she felt the gentle pressure of his hand. He did not take his eyes off her face.

That is where their parents found them when they arrived just before dawn. Caleb had not left his vigil. His mother, giving a small gasp, went straight to him and put her arms around him, her tears wetting his hair.

Jo's parents went immediately to the other side of the bed. Alice, her eyes bright with unshed tears, kissed her daughter's cheek.

Caleb's father placed his hand on his son's shoulders. He couldn't fathom the pain his son was going through at this moment.

They gently convinced Caleb he needed to get some rest or they would have to have him admitted for exhaustion. He tried to argue with them. He swayed as he stood up, giving truth to his exhaustion. He leaned over and gave his wife a kiss on the forehead. "I love you," he whispered. The Collins stayed at their daughter's bed side. Brenda and David accompanied their son to his apartment.

Icthus

Chapter Thirty-six

Caleb woke up and was looking out the window. He barely recalled getting back to the apartment. He turned over to stare at the pillow that normally held Jo's head. His parent's had taken the spare bedroom. Mom and Dad C. were still at the hospital.

He could smell coffee and heard movement. At least one of his parents was also up. He looked at the clock. It showed him it was just past nine. He only slept a couple of hours. He swung his legs around and sat up. He hoped this was all some nightmare from which he would awaken. He knew that wasn't the case.

He stood up and made his way to the bathroom.

When he finally entered the kitchen, his mother was sipping from a steaming mug. She motioned for him to sit down. She got up and went to the cupboard to get him a mug. She filled it with the hot coffee and set it down before him.

"How did you sleep?" His mother asked.

He shrugged. "I'm surprised I slept at all. Even then it was only a couple of hours."

He sipped the coffee absently and stared out the window beside the dining table. Brenda remained silent. She understood he was pre-occupied: still attempting to process the shocking turn his life had taken and allowed him to work through it.

He finished the coffee and stood up to go back to his room to change and return to the hospital.

By the time he showered and dressed, his dad was awake and sitting in the living room watching the news. Occasionally he would pick up the mug on the end table beside him and take a sip.

Caleb was impatient to get back to Jo. His parents sensing his mood were quick to tidy up and they left together.

They drove to the hospital and stood silently as the elevator whisked them to the floor where Jo's room was.

Not much changed from the few hours they were gone. Jo looked much the same: heavily bandaged head, tubes and wires attached to her. He couldn't see the bruise on her face when she fell.

Mom C. was dozing in the chair Caleb had vacated. Dad C. was seated by the window, a Styrofoam cup in his hand, staring blankly out the window. The movement of them entering the room caught his attention and he stood up, taking a sip from the cup and grimaced. "Hospital coffee is bad at the best of times, but it is particularly gross when it's cold."

He came over to where Caleb was standing and clasped his shoulder. "She is still heavily sedated. She was awake for a few minutes and then drifted off again. The nurses say she is doing fine and should be more wakeful by this afternoon. Well, at least until they come and give her more medication. She probably won't be fully aware until tomorrow."

Caleb nodded, not attempting to speak as he worked to bring his emotions under a semblance of control.

David had managed to scrounge up a couple of extra chairs and placed them around the bed so they could be comfortable while they waited for Jo to wake up.

Alice's head slipped and she jerked awake. She rearranged herself and apologized to them. Brenda smiled. "That's not necessary dear. It's been a long night. At least we had the luxury of a bed for a couple of hours or I would be doing the same thing. Now that we're here, you guys should head over to the apartment and get some rest yourself."

Alice hesitated, torn between the desire to get a bit of rest and not wanting to leave her daughter's side. Caleb looked at his in-laws. "It's not a bad idea. You guys probably had about the same amount of rest I did. We will be here if anything changes. It is only about 20 minutes away."

He knelt down beside his mother-in-law and gave her a hug. "I know it's hard, but I don't want you passing out and giving yourself a concussion." He gave a lopsided grin. "Imagine when she wakes up and sees you with a bandaged head in the next bed?"

She chuckled, glanced over to her husband and nodded her agreement. "It's almost noon now. We will go and get freshened up and be back in a few hours. Besides, you know how cranky Bob gets when he doesn't get real coffee."

The Collins left and the Whites began their vigil. Caleb had been in contact with the office, updated them on Jo's condition and had them forward any business he needed to take care of to his home phone where he would check on it later.

Jo pretty much slept the rest of the day. She woke up occasionally and smiled at Caleb. "I love you. "she murmured before drifting off to sleep once again.

Dr. Phroneo stopped and checked her progress. She smiled and expressed her pleasure meeting Caleb's parents. She assured them Jo was recovering nicely and made arrangements to meet with them and the oncologist tomorrow and bid them a nice day.

The Collins returned to the hospital mid-afternoon, better for a chance to shower and change into clean clothes. Jo was not yet aware they were with her.

Icthus

The family stayed until visiting hours were over. Since it was no longer an emergency, the duty nurse reluctantly shoed them out, but told them they could come back after nine am.

Chapter Thirty-seven

Jo was sitting up when they arrived later that afternoon. Caleb smiled and hurried over to kiss her. "I always wondered what I would look like wearing a turban. What do you think?"

He smiled. "You could go bald and I will still love you."

She gave a small laugh. "Well that's good, because I am!"

"How's the head? I should take advantage of it and really look into the mind of a woman."

She smiled and laid her head back on the pillow, feeling like it was too heavy to hold up any longer. "I don't think so," she responded. "I have to keep some secrets you know."

She noticed her parents and gave an exclamation of delight. She held out her arms and they went to her giving her a big hug. "You didn't have to come, you know. But I'm glad you did."

Her father straightened up and smiled. Jo could see the worried look in his eyes. "I had no choice. Your mother threatened to walk if I didn't call the airlines and book the next available flight."

Mrs. Collins was gripping her daughter's hand; tears bright in her eyes. "My baby."

Alice released her from her hug and stood back. Jo noticed her In-laws. "Mom and Dad W! Thank-you for coming."

Brenda went to the bedside and gave her a kiss on the cheek. "Oh, honey, we had to be here for the both of you."

Jo shifted uncomfortably in her bed. She was embarrassed by the attention, Caleb could tell. "Oh, come on. You don't need to make such a big fuss over this. I'm sure everything will turn out all right."

She looked at their stricken faces and started to cry. It wasn't going to be all right. Caleb went over to her and sat on the bed and held her close. "Dr. Phroneo and the oncologist will be in after lunch to talk to us."

He looked at Jo and then at their parents. "We would like you to be there with us as well."

They voiced their consent that they would do whatever the couple needed from them in support.

Doctor Phroneo arrived shortly after one with the oncologist whom he introduced as Doctor Roberts. They smiled at everyone in the room and Caleb introduced their parents.

Doctor Roberts looked over the chart and then at Jo and Caleb. "I'm not going to sugar coat this. It is a challenge to knock out the cancer at your stage. There are four stages, from the most treatable stage one, to what we consider life-threatening, stage four. Sometime between stages three and four is when most cancer cells migrate to other parts of the body where they grow uncontrollably.

"Unfortunately, the cancer you have is one of the more aggressive ones. You are already at stage four."

Mrs. Collins gasped and reached for her husband's hand. Caleb and Jo looked at each other and then back to the doctor.

"I don't want you to get the wrong idea here. I am not telling you to wrap up your affairs and go home to die. That is certainly an option.

"What I'm saying is it makes our treatment options more limited. We usually recommend a combination of chemotherapy and radiation: Sometimes used together, or one course following the other.

"Both options alone or in combination have side effects ranging from nausea, loss of appetite, temporary hair loss and sometimes mild burns from the radiation. Surgery is not an option. The tumor is in a location which is too difficult to excise without the risk of brain damage."

Doctor Roberts went over all of their options. He patiently answered their questions and concerns about the various medications that she would require to start fighting this disease and when they could expect to see if the regime was working to reduce the size of the tumor.

He offered no guarantees of the success of the treatment. They were already aware the odds of successful treatment were not good. "We should know within the first four weeks if the treatment will have any effect. We have made great strides in treating cancers in the brain, but it has a natural barrier which makes it resistant to a lot of very good drugs."

He indicated treatment would start in the next few days. If she responded well to the initial round then she would be allowed to go home where she could return as an outpatient.

She was also scheduled for a battery of tests to determine if the cancer was localized in one area or if it had metastasized to other parts of the body. Dr. Roberts held out little hope the cancer had not spread. It was rare for late stage cancers to still be localized in one part of the body. The tests over the next few days would tell the rest of the story.

Icthus

Chapter Thirty-eight

It turned out they had mere months instead of years ahead of them. Jo did not respond well to treatment. She was violently ill from the chemicals they had injected her with to combat the disease.

The anti-nauseau medication they administered before each treatment seemed like a joke to her. She spent hours with her head over a bucket.

The radiation burned her scalp. She wept when she saw her long hair was gone.

Her mother and mother-in-law stayed at the apartment with her and drove her to the hospital so Caleb could return to work. Not that he was able to do much, with his mind constantly on his wife.

Most evenings they would take turns bathing Jo's forehead with damp cold clothes. The headaches did not diminish, although the pain medication did take the edge off.

It was a long month with the almost daily visits to the hospital for treatment or testing to chart the progress of the disease. It was apparent the treatment was having little effect on halting its progress.

At their parent's suggestion, he took a leave of absence from work, closed up the apartment and took Jo home to die.

Winter faded to spring as Jo's life faded from this world. The weather warmed up and they would sit in the Collins's wooden Adirondack chairs savoring the clean country air. Caleb only left her side when one of their parents or friends from the church would stop by to give him a break.

Icthus

He would take a shower, layed down for half an hour, grab a sandwich and something to drink, then be back beside his wife. They talked quietly when Jo was able to and he would hold a bottle of water or juice for her while she sipped on its contents through a straw. When she didn't feel like talking, he would hold her hand and read a book to her.

Jo was sleeping more than she was awake. The medication to control the pain and the disease ravaged her body was preparing to release her soul back to its Maker and Lord.

The family held a subdued celebration for their sixth anniversary. Only the family, Doc and his wife were in attendance.

They had prepared themselves for her eventual admittance to the Local hospice, but that was not to be.

He was holding her in his arms on the night of their sixth anniversary. She cuddled against his body and smiled. "So nice," she mumbled.

Caleb just held her. "Cal, It's so beautiful!" she sighed, closed her eyes and was gone.

He cradled her body against him, his tears bathing her head and wetting her newly grown hair. His sobs alerted their parents to that something had happened. As soon as they walked into the room they knew.

Brenda and Alice started to weep and went to be with their children. His father, barely able to contain his own emotions, pulled out his cell phone to activate the chapel's prayer chain. Jo's father approached the bed and gently placed his hands on his wife's shoulders.

Within a few minutes members of the chapel family began to arrive at the house. Because her death occurred at home the police were notified and the coroner summoned.

Caleb felt frozen. He watched as the coroner quickly examined Jo and made the pronouncement.

He followed the gurney with her body out to the hearse, which would take her to the funeral home. All those arrangements had been made. He followed the vehicle to the road and watched it as it disappeared around the bend.

He continued to stand on the side of the road until his father came out and gently guided him back to the house.

Justin made it back in time for the funeral. Caleb requested his presence as a pall bearer and Justin obtained emergency leave to be able to accept the honors. He was fortunate that he happened to be in the country.

He stood beside his friend during the visitation and took the lead position on the right side of the coffin which held Jo's earthy remains. The last time he was with his friends was on the day of their wedding.

He stood opposite Caleb at the graveside with the other pall bearers. He could barely see for the tears coursing down his face. He was burying someone he considered to be not only his friend but his sister.

Justin realized Caleb's faith was shaken to the core. Justin had long ago turned his back on God and religion. His line of work had further alienated him from anywhere near a conscience and what the civilized world would consider ethical or moral.

As the Doc finished the graveside service, Justin wondered how deeply this would affect Caleb. This time he had a twelve pack in the trunk of his rented car.

Icthus

Chapter Thirty-nine

It was September when Caleb decided to return to their apartment in Toronto. He took the summer off with the blessing of his boss to give him a chance to come to terms with Jo's death.

His parents attempted to persuade him to move back to Goulais River. This was his home. With the advances in technology, he could do his job regardless of where he chose to live. Although he was tempted to stay, in the end he wanted to go back to their place.

He knew Jo was no longer a physical part of his life but he needed to return to the place where they had made their home. This is where his memories were still strong and he wanted to remember her. He had made a few quick trips throughout the summer, touching base with his boss and making sure the dust didn't overtake the rooms of the apartment.

He arrived early in the evening. It was starting to get dark and he turned on the lamps in the living room. He was really by himself for the first time in nearly three months. He picked up a picture of them taken on a trip to Edmonton the first year they were married. They spent the day exploring the West Edmonton Mall: at one time the largest shopping center in North America. It was Polaroid, taken of them, holding and petting a lion cub.

He smiled as he remembered that day. They roamed the mall from one end to the other and back. They stood on the pirate ship and took a submarine ride. The water park was tempting, but they decided to wait for the next trip they made.

They eventually ended up at the amusement park and its triple-loop roller coaster. A sign posted on a pole boasted it was world's largest indoor triple-loop. The main hill was an astounding ten stories tall, or over one hundred feet.

He had to laugh as he remembered Jo keeping her eyes tightly closed as they made the assent up that first hill. The cars moved slowly and she finally opened her eyes. "Well, this isn't so bad..."

She let out a scream as the cars suddenly seemed to drop straight down. When they got off he was laughing and she punched his shoulder. She vowed never to ride any roller coaster again.

He put the picture down and continued his trip down memory lane. She was not one for collecting bric a brac and liked to have everything in its place. He ran his fingers along the book shelf and pulled out a photo album. It was filled with pictures of her.

She was standing on the top observation pod of the CN tower. He was surprised that for someone who regularly climbed trees as a child, he had a bout of vertigo looking down to the base of the tower over one thousand feet below. Jo laughed as he glued himself to the inside wall and worked his way back to the elevator.

He opened the closet and saw that her clothes were still hanging there, including her wedding dress, safely stored in its garment bag. Jo had hoped to someday pass it on to a daughter: a dream that would now not be fulfilled. He closed the door and sat on the side of the bed they once shared. He picked up her pillow and inhaled her scent. He hugged it to himself to muffle the sobs.

Chapter Forty

The next day he returned to his office. Jen saw him first and jumped up from her desk and ran over to him. Giving him big hug she smiled, "I am sure glad you're back. For good, I hope?"

Caleb nodded, "Maybe. I am not going to make any big changes right now. Is Dave here? I wasn't planning on coming in today but I wanted to touch base."

He looked around the office. Other coworkers had noticed him and were waving and shouting out welcomes. He smiled and nodded and turned his attention back to his assistant. "It has been five months since I've been here full time. You haven't given my office to anybody else yet, have you?"

She laughed and directed him to his office. "It is all yours, just the way you left it."

He opened the door and walked in. "I think it's neater, you have been housekeeping. Thank-you."

Jen grinned. "Well a little dusting and watering the fern. I'll let Dave know you're here." She closed the door behind her as she left the room, leaving Caleb with his thoughts.

He sat down at Is desk and couldn't help but thinking back to that fateful February day when the world as he knew it came to an end. He felt hollow inside: like someone took a melon scoop and scraped him out. He wondered if he would ever stop aching for Jo's touch once more.

He supposed with time, he would be able to think of his wife without the intense sorrow that accompanied those thoughts. The wound was still very raw.

He stared out of the window. He was correct in what he said to Jen; he wasn't going to make any major changes in his life. He needed time to heal and think about what the next move would be.

The intercom buzzed and broke his reverie. He acknowledged it and Jen's voice floated into the room. "Dave said he will be free in about 15 minutes and will come here. Since technically you aren't officially here there is less chance of being interrupted."

He thanked Jen and continued to stare out of the window until he heard the door open again.

Chapter Forty-one

Life slowly started to take on the shape of some sort of normality. Caleb no longer felt overwhelming grief when he thought of Jo. By Christmas he managed to empty the closets and cupboards of her clothing.

He flew home for the holiday, and quietly spent the time with his parents. He still considered him-self a part of the Collins family. They did not dissuade him of the idea and welcomed him with open arms and tears.

He missed Jo terribly as it was one of her favorite holidays. She always went way overboard in the decoration department. Even though they usually went home to celebrate with their families, she turned the apartment into a riotous display of garland, tinsel and lights. She spent hours looking for the perfect tree, which seemed to fill half the living room.

He kept her collection of Anne McCaffery novels, because they used to be his. He also kept the cookbooks.

She loved to try out new recipes and she would work her way through various cook books until she had tried every recipe at least once. She made notations in the margins as to which dishes she would do again as well as those which she indicated would not see the light of her kitchen again.

He read some of the comments in the margins and briefly wondered why she hadn't become a chef instead of a teacher. He asked her once and she laughed and said this was a hobby. If she had to do it for a living, she would hate it.

It was almost a year before he started to attend the Assembly again. He came to realize God was watching over him even though he spent most of the first year after Jo's death immersed in work or laying on the couch in the depths of a depression which was part of the healing process. He also spent much time venting his anger at God for taking her away from him.

When Caleb sat at the Lord's Supper for that first time, he felt he was finally coming home and could truly look towards the future.

He had several discussions about what direction he would like to take with the company. Since he no longer had ties to keep him in Toronto, he took up Dave's long standing offer to spend time in the companies' offices around the world.

Caleb kept the apartment as his base when in Toronto and would spend anywhere from two or three weeks to months working out of the country. His job description changed to trouble shooting software and hardware issues, as well overseeing new product launches in the various countries.

He lived this semi-nomadic life for the next ten years. He rarely made it home to visit family. Sometimes they would join him, staying with him at the company provided accommodations.

He took advantage of the locations he was stationed to do quite a bit of site-seeing. He often thought of Jo and how much she would have loved to these countries. They had done some travelling together and had planned to do more. He spent time exploring Europe, Asia, Africa, Australia and South America.

The most profound trip he made was to the Israel, the birthplace of his Savior. Jo would have been filled with wonderment as the stood in the places where Jesus stood and lived almost two thousand years before.

He was moved to tears as he stood on Mount Calvary where his salvation was paid for with the blood of the Creator of the Universe. He felt a sense of awe when he viewed the tomb, traditionally viewed as the grave site which failed to hold that man captive.

He was building quite a financial portfolio as well. Another five or six years and he would be able to retire and maybe pursue another career.

Perhaps he would turn his attention to sharing the knowledge he had acquired to some of the faith organizations working to promote the cause of Christ around the world.

It was during this time he became acquainted with house churches. Some of the countries he visited or worked in were not as open to the freedom to worship as he was accustomed to in Canada.

Churches were controlled by the state and unable to freely preach the gospel, or were outlawed. People who named the name of Christ subjected to intense persecution.

Like their New Testament brethren, the brothers and sisters met privately in homes to break bread together in worship and fellowship. What surprised Caleb was the fervor of these people. Their faith was truly being tested in the fire and they were shining gold.

Caleb though long on that perspective. In the western world, the church was not effective: lulled into a false sense of security. Peace was dangerous to its existence. Christians in Canada and other western countries were ignorant of the dangers in the world.

He also thought of Justin periodically through this time. When he made it back home he would pay a call on Mrs. Jones and catch up on the news. He occasionally met up with Justin, when his leave coincided with his visits. Sometimes they would be in the same part of the world. They would spend an evening bringing each other up to date.

To Caleb, Justin often looked distracted. They would share details of their lives from the last time they got together. He would listen to Justin and think that this was some polished and rehearsed recital.

Caleb noticed he would often glance up to the left, something Caleb learned meant a person was not being truthful. He noticed his friend had lost the easy bearing he used to have. He was careful, almost assessing and calculating. There was a tenseness about him; he was like a tightly wound spring. But then almost twenty years had passed since they floated lazily down the river on their inner tubes.

Caleb had long ago stopped attempting to bring up spiritual matters with Justin. He would slough off Caleb's questions and steer the conversation away from that aspect of his life.

Caleb realized a sense of sadness and loss. Justin had slipped away almost as surely as Jo had. The only difference was Justin was still alive.

Where there was life, Caleb reasoned, there would also be hope. He left the matter in the hands of the One who could make a difference.

Chapter Forty-two

"Ok, let's continue our study on what the Bible says about being an extreme Christian."

It had been nearly twelve years since he last conducted a Bible study: since before Jo's graduation to glory. It surprised him to realize so much time passed.

He had worked the wanderlust out of his life and was no longer employed in a fulltime capacity as a troubleshooter for the company he had been with for over fifteen years. He started his own consulting company: taking only those projects which interested him.

The years of travelling and seeing how his brothers and sisters in Christ lived in other parts of the world gave him an eye-opening education to the spiritual struggles going on in the world. His faith was strengthened and he developed a world view of the church that he would not have otherwise had.

Caleb was convinced it was only a matter of time before the persecutions he witnessed in other parts of the world would come here to comfortable Canada. Some of his peers scoffed at the idea, but some listened and like Caleb started preparing for it.

"Last week we finished studying what made Daniel such an outstanding example of having assurance in God. Does anyone have any questions or observations before we continue with a new lesson?"

Caleb looked around the table. People seemed to be shaking their heads. "Great! Now let's take a look at the life of Paul and what it takes for him to be a committed Christian. Let's turn in our books to page two hundred and thirty-nine." Who would like to start reading?"

Shelia started to read. "I like the word zealous. It is a cool, old-fashioned word. Straight out of Webster's dictionary we read: *full of, characterized by, or showing zeal; ardently devoted to a purpose; fervent; enthusiastic.* Paul, the focus of this particular study, describes himself as a person who was very zealous in what he did."

They worked their way through the first part of the lesson. The group discovered what Paul was a zealous Pharisee, persecuting the young church. He then experienced Christ on the road to Damascus where he was looking for the hated Christians.

Paul was a changed man, but he was still a zealous and committed man. His allegiance changed from a staunch supporter of the Law and maintaining the Jewish lifestyle from the people of the Way, to being one of the strongest advocates for Jesus Christ in the early first century.

Caleb led the discussion and they decided to call it a night after they had shared their conclusions on the words the author of the study had included as an overall part of the study.

He enjoyed these types of studies, because it made people think and taught them vital Bible study skills which were sadly lacking in many mainstream churches. Most people who call themselves Christian tended to only play the part on Sunday mornings. They were more interested in socializing or listening to the good music, maybe even had a speaker that could communicate effectively to the audience.

But from Monday to Saturday, their Bibles gathered dust on the shelves in their houses or served as holders for the remote controls.

Caleb encouraged members of the small gropup to actually study the Bible. He believed the story that if you give a man a fish he will eat for a day, but if you teach a man to fish, he will never go hungry again. The same principal applied to spiritual sustenance.

"How important is it to be totally committed to Jesus Christ?"

He waited silently while the members of the group wrestled with the best way to answer the question. He had to admit it wasn't something the average Sunday-go-to church person gave much thought about. Cameron spoke up. "Perhaps it means that if we commit to Christ we should give it our best shot."

Caleb nodded. "That's sounds reasonable. Does someone have something else to say about commitment?"

"It's like supporting a sports team," suggested Sarah. "I mean, think about the fans in the stand. They are totally committed to the success of that team. They come dressed in the team's colors, cheer them on, sometimes chewing them out if they are playing a bad game that night. They get after the referees for making bad calls. It doesn't matter if the team is bad or good, they support it no matter what."

Caleb thought about that one for a minute. "Good points. So to sum it up we are talking about an attitude of total support and giving our all. Does that sound about right so far?"

Heads nodded around the table. He continued. "What the impact of our commitment to Jesus Christ? What are the results of such an attitude?"

He looked around the table as the group members considered the new question. "Let me give you an example from my own childhood. Is that ok with everybody?"

"I recently heard a story about the old pastor of the church I grew up in.

"His Name was Samuel Johnson. I knew him as The Doctor or just plain Doc. He had earned a Doctor of Theology degree from

Dallas Theological Seminary and had come to Northern Ontario to start a Bible College in our very rural community of Goulais River.

"I was speaking to a man named Rick. Rick had at one time owned a furniture store in town and Doc would sometimes drop in to say hello. Rick said that one day they were talking about how God works and was told this following story.

"For the sake of brevity, I am going to shorten it up a bit."

People chuckled at his comments about being brief. He usually was, allowing other people equal time at the table, even though he was the group leader. "Rick," said Doc. "I build churches. I go out to the plot of land and lay out the spot for the building and start digging the foundations.

"People would come by and ask what I was doing. I would tell them I was building a church. They would say, 'Are you crazy? You don't have the money to build a church.'

"I would reply, 'The Lord wants me to build a church. If He wants me to stop, then the money will stop coming in.'

"Then Rick said Doc told him, "You know, I always had something to do on that building. The money would keep coming in until the church was built, then it would stop."

"Now what does this mean to a nine-year old boy?" He looked at the people as they shrugged their shoulders. Absolutely nothing.

"I was nine-years old when I first met Doc. It was during Vacation Bible School at the newly formed North Woods Bible Chapel campus, which consisted of 70 acres of land, a farm house, a small cabin, a barn and a few utility sheds. There was a hole in the ground where the foundations were being laid for a building that would serve the new church family which was meeting in the farm house kitchen.

"Doc stood in the middle of a circle of fidgety children with a smile on his face as he welcomed us that first morning. He was dressed in jeans, plaid shirt and a beat up old straw hat. He called us "Mohicans."

Eyebrows shot up in surprise. "Yeah, today someone would call him on that for being degrogatory. But he used it as a term of endearment.

"Of course we had no idea what that meant. We sang John 3:16, which none of us new. Our classroom was in the hay loft in the barn.

"Now to a nine year old boy, Vacation Bible School was something else. We went on hikes, had horseback rides, a hayride, and a treasure hunt on the last day that had us running over half the property.

"We heard the Bible stories, memorized Scripture and were encouraged to bring friends for the contest. At the end of the week, we went home with the wooden matchstick crosses we made for our craft, a workbook that we had done during the week and an invitation to come to something called Sunday school.

"Our Sunday school class was held in the barn until it got too cold and then we spent the winter at one of the member's houses. The chapel building was ready for use the next spring and we moved into it for our Sunday meetings.

"It was during the fall in the back corner classroom that my life changed forever. It was there during my Sunday school class that I gave my life to Christ.

"What makes the story more poignant is North Woods Bible Chapel was the last church Doc built.

"Not only that, he wanted to build a Bible College. The College operated out of the same buildings the chapel did. During the week it was a Christian training center and on the weekend it was a place for the brethren get together to worship.

"Doc, led by his commitment to provide quality Bible training, not only to young people to make them able ministers, he also built one last church were he spent the remainder of his life ministering at.

"The questioned I asked myself and I'm asking you today is this: What is your level of commitment to what you believe?

"To a nine-year old boy, that commitment caused a life-changing experience. How many nine-year olds will say the same of you?"

He stopped talking and watched the faces of the people seated around the table. He knew that he had given them something to think about during the coming week.

"Jason, would close our session tonight in prayer?"

"This was a really good study tonight," Caleb told the group. "We had some good discussion. Next week we are going to pick up where we left off by sharing what Paul's testimonies revealed about him and his message. More importantly, we will get an insight into how one of the most successful church planters presented the gospel to various people across a variety of cultures."

"Thank you for coming. You guys are working hard with this study and it's paying off."

He drove home to his apartment. He flicked on the lights as he entered the doorway and walked over to the window which gave him a panoramic vista of the cityscape.

The view had changed greatly since he and Jo first moved there. A sleepy suburb of Toronto had grown into a thriving city in its own right. Several years ago, the provincial government passed legislation amalgamating the smaller communities into the metropolis known as GTA: the Greater Toronto Area.

He had not seen the need to relocate. With the constant traveling it became a place to land until the next assignment. Five years ago he did purchase a house on Sand Bay near where he grew up. He generally spent summers there. Situated on the Eastern side of Lake Superior, he would sit on the deck and view some spectacular sunsets: colors not only blazing the sky, but reflected on the evening waters of the world's largest freshwater lake.

He walked over to his desk and flipped through the pages of his schedule. He stopped at May and reassured himself when he the Victoria Day Weekend brightly circled in red with an exclamation mark. The day he left for the north and his retreat on Sand Bay. He smiled as he turned off the lights and headed for bed. He may even do some fishing this summer. Dad would like that.

Icthus

Chapter Forty-three

"Hey, Major!" Justin paused briefly when he realized that it was himself being addressed. He turned and saw the team he had worked with so closely for over ten years grinning at him and saluting.

He was getting used to the new title and the clusters on his shoulder that marked his promotion. He grinned back and returned the salute. This was his family. They had been through crap of which the normal world had no concept of. "At ease, gentlemen."

He walked over to them and accepted their congratulations. "Well, what do we call you now?" the newly promoted Captain Barry asked. "It's like we can't call you Cap anymore."

Justin laughed and slapped Barry on the back. "Nope, that's your handle now. We will have to think of something. Meet you all at the Canteen at twenty hundred?"

They all nodded in the affirmative and dispersed. Usually there didn't have to be a reason to drink, but this was a special occasion. Promotions in their field were hard won, and rare as the lifespan of operatives was not considered long. Justin had beaten the odds and had been with Special Operations for close to fifteen years: a lifetime in the espionage business. Justin knew only too well the pain of colleagues not returning home after the mission.

He arrived at his quarters and looked at the clock eighteen hundred, or six o'clock in the evening. He had two hours before he met with his team.

He picked up the phone and called his mother. She was now retired from her career as a teacher and was learning things she never had time to before. One of those things had been skydiving. "Are you crazy?" he asked her when she told him she was taking lessons.

"It's something I've always wanted to do," she said. "We decided to do it right after we went bungee jumping at the Royal Gorge in British Colombia."

He could feel his eyebrows do the Spock thing and disappear into is hair line. "Bungee jumping? Retired teachers are supposed to sip tea and add to their collection of cats."

Mrs. Jones laughed, "Oh, Justin, that is so twenty or thirty years ago. Besides you skydive."

"Yeah, mom and I'm twenty-five years younger than you are."

He could not persuade her to change her mind and resigned himself to the real possibility he would be burying his mother in a jam jar.

"This is Carol. I'm out enjoying my retirement. Leave a message."

Justin left a message and hung up. She would call him later and he would share his news.

He stripped out of his uniform and carelessly tossed it on the bed. He glanced up and looked at himself in the mirror. He had his close calls. There were scars from more than a few knife attacks and he had also been shot a few times. He was not a vain man, but he was proud of the shape he was in. In his business, you had to be at the top of your game, mentally, and physically.

He could outperform recruits less than half his age. There was at least one per training session who would attempt to put him to the test. He noticed his hair was shot with grey and he could discern the beginning of lines along his eyes.

He supposed if he wanted to he could continue with the field operations for a couple of more years. However with his background and knowledge, His Superior officers may want to move him into strategic planning.

He turned from the mirror and headed into the bathroom and a hot shower. Tonight was going to be a wild party.

Icthus

Chapter Forty-four

Caleb was not surprised when the federal government announced it was implementing the War Measures Act and stripped Canadians of their basic rights.

Months of world economic crisis's, which was precipitated by the sub-mortgage lending craze of the late twentieth and early twenty-first century, backfired in 2005 causing a cascade of bank failures. In a matter of months, real estate lost much of its inflated value in the United States for a period of several years.

Caleb was fortunate being in Canada. Stricter banking and lending laws buffered much of that. The deepening debt crisis spiraled out of control in the States and then to Europe. The Euro crunch of 2011-2013 was another factor In the spiraling downturn in the economy.

Caleb had seen the beginnings of this. He slowly divested his portfolio of stocks, bonds and foreign currency, converting them into precious metals and cash.

He had no confidence in the banking sector in Canada, and did not keep a lot of investments tied up. He also had several real estate investments around the country, and worked to consolidate everything and keep his assets as liquid as possible.

Lingering drought conditions in the bread basket regions of many countries, including Canada, caused reduced or failed crops. Prices for even basic food items rose sharply. In third world countries millions were starving. Even in developed countries like Canada, many people were experiencing hunger for the first time in their lives.

Line ups at food banks and soup kitchens grew even longer, stretching already thin resources beyond the breaking point. Often times they would be forced to close their doors early, running out of food. Many did not reopen those doors.

Caleb had followed the logic and with the help of the Elders in his Asssembly in Toronto and in Goulais had stockpiled food stores to help their members. Caleb had also stockpiled supplies mainly at his summer residence. He reasoned that when the dam broke, he and maybe a few others would find relative safety away from the urban centers.

People grew more desperate. Mass riots broke out. Rumors of a supply of flour at a local store caused a stampede of hungry people to mob the building. Store workers, terrified, locked the doors fearing for their safety.

Police were called out and were unable to control the angry crowd as they no longer were interested in obtaining food, but were looking to take out their collective frustrations.

Windows were smashed at the businesses all over the down town shopping district. Cars were overturned and set ablaze. It wasn't only happening in Toronto but in every major city in the country and around the world. Caleb watched the madness from his apartment window. He could hear the screams of people and the fires set by the looters.

Within forty-eight hours the government had declared a state of emergency and called out the military to restore order.

The rioters were rounded up and taken to detention centers. Curfews were strictly enforced and soldiers had the authority to arrest citizens without due process. Public gatherings were outlawed.

It did not matter the reasons for the gathering. Many churches closed as the militia forced themselves into Sunday services and removed protesting worshippers to waiting trucks and busses.

People who feared being attacked by looters and thieves now walked in fear of their own government. Federal and provincial governments nationalized financial institutions and major corporations in an effort to restore some sort of order.

Caleb, as one of the foremost IT engineers in the world, was encouraged to lend his talents to supporting the greater cause. He smiled and said that should not be a problem.

 The government was willing to pay him more than is customary fees and allowed him the security access needed to carry out such a task.

What his new employers did not realize was Caleb was not interested in carrying out their agenda. He had one of his own.

Icthus

Chapter Forty-five

Justin was sitting at his desk going over the various reports. He was surprised with the extent of the powers the counter terrorism unit had been granted in the wake of the current crisis. He spent a long time in the shadowy world of Black Ops: where nothing was clear cut and they were a law unto themselves.

His organization was charged to do what was necessary to maintain the security of the nation. They now had the power to use the same procedures on any Canadian citizen labeled as subversive by the government.

Any opposition to the government was a threat to the peace and sovereignty of the Dominion. To Justin it didn't matter if they were street rioters or church goers. His teams would deal with them equally and with extreme prejudice if necessary.

He rarely went on missions himself. He was assigned to urban control and had twenty teams under his command. They broke up everything from bar brawls to food riots to prayer meetings. All public gatherings were illegal.

Many of the unit members felt uneasy at first when they were required to disband seemingly innocent meetings, like church meetings. There were protests about people's violations of their rights. They quickly died in the face of extreme force being used upon them by the squads of trained soldiers in full riot gear.

Church goers for the most part were not fighters.

He stood up, stretched and walked over to the window which overlooked the downtown business sector of Greater Toronto. What normally would have been a bustling street, filled with automobiles, street cars and buses and sidewalks, filled with hurrying people was a virtual ghost town. From this height he could see some people walking the street, but they were no longer hurrying back to work or heading off to lunch or a bit of shopping.

When he was on the street, people walked, shoulders hunched, looking furtively around, afraid they were being followed. He shook his head and gave a rueful grin. They looked at his uniform and quickened their pace.

Justin knew there was no reason to waste resources on physically following people, not with the GPS tracking chips that would soon be mandatory for all citizens.

Of course there would be those who would not cooperate with the government's agenda. Justin's profession taught him there was always an undercurrent to any society. Whether it was organized crime, or those who fell through the cracks, they would soon not be an issue with the new world order. All would be eventually rounded up and their anti-government activities quietly removed from society.

He wondered what Caleb's response was to all of these changes happening in society. The last time he met with him was at a restaurant in Ottawa where he was working on an assignment for the company he was working for.

They spoke of what they had been doing since the last time they were together and a little bit about their childhood antics. They laughed over the time they were spying on the work going on one summer in their beloved gravel pit. They accidentally disturbed a hive of bees and in the scramble to get away from the angry insects Caleb tripped over his bike and broke his arm.

Justin was waiting for Caleb to give him the obligatory attempt to encourage him to come back to God - but it never happened. He thought that perhaps his friend had finally come to the conclusion that it was a waste of his time.

Icthus

He knew Caleb eventually renewed his faith after Jo's death. It had taken time, but he grew stronger and continued to be active in the church. He kept his eyes open for his friend's name to appear on the roster of people arrested for illegal activities, but it never appeared.

Justin breathed a sigh of relief. Maybe his friend grew smart in the face of the recent world alignment and realized he had been wrong about all this religious crap.

One of the reports caught his attention. The operative had gotten wind of a small group of people meeting in a house. They had managed to infiltrate the group and discovered it was a group of Christians.

The operative took no action against the group of people as technically it was not a public gathering. He submitted the report with a request for a follow up.

This was an interesting development. They closed the churches and the churches moved into houses. He tagged the report for clarification from his superiors on how to proceed with these small groups. He would not be surprised to find those types of meetings would also be deemed subversive to the state and ordered to be shut down with extreme prejudice.

He queried his database for Caleb. He discovered he was on contract by the government to oversee security of their computer systems. Justin read Caleb had a security clearance on par with his own. He also discovered Caleb was considered one of the foremost Information Technology experts in the world.

Justin raised his eyebrows at Caleb's qualifications. He knew his friend as a smart man. Caleb didn't talk much about his job and certainly not how he was perceived by his peers in the Information Technology sector.

Justin was surprised Caleb turned his back on his faith and

worked for the very institution that was trying to exterminate that group of people called Christians.

He shrugged and returned to his desk. Maybe it was time to give his old friend a call and get together for supper and catch up.

Chapter Forty-six

Far from turning his back on his faith, Caleb was busy encouraging believers at every opportunity.

He thought the best way to hide from the enemy was in plain sight. By day he went to his government appointed office. He kept the computers running and the information highway flowing and secure.

His access to government data and his security clearance put him in a unique position to be able to pass on warnings to the brothers and sister if they were targets or if their cell locations had been compromised.

With Caleb's assistance and others who also worked secretly within the government, the Church reorganized and became invisible to as much official scrutiny as possible.

After the original arrests, Government forces were capturing fewer subversives. The assumption being most had been rounded up and detained in the re-education centers.

Intense propaganda campaigns had worked to restore order and confidence in the actions the government took to contain the crisis. People were encouraged to report any suspicious behavior to the authorities.

Unofficially vigilantism was the new policy of the day. Law abiding citizens were allowed to stop suspicious behavior themselves. Caleb witnessed swarms descend upon brothers attempting to share the gospel of Jesus Christ, beating them into silence.

Police and soldiers would eventually break up the swarm, only to prevent them from turning their attentions to the innocent.

Everything was under control.

That was the official party line and the powers that be congratulated themselves on a job well done.

Quite to the contrary: the Church was not only healthy but flourishing in Canada in a way it had not done for decades.

The persecutions faced on a daily basis quickly burned away the dross of the world. People were hungry for spiritual things and they took advantage of that hunger to spread the good news of Jesus Christ.

Caleb left the office for the day. He returned to his apartment to eat a quick meal. After washing up the dishes he would leave a light the the television on to make it seem like he was still there.

He left his vehicle in the parking garage; it was much too expensive for fuel to use it on a daily basis. He used the transit system to travel around the city.

On any given night, the church gathered together. It was too dangerous for people to meet together as one large group on one day of the week. With Churches closed and public gatherings outlawed, different ways of gathering were devised.

So they met in groups of no larger than ten or fifteen people. Caleb joined a group of men who had taken it upon themselves to shepherd some of these groups. They were the only ones who knew the extent of the network but then not all were aware of the locations of each group.

It was during this massive social engineering exercise Caleb came across a back door security breach in one of the computer systems. He would not have noticed it at all if it hadn't been for some blips that had popped up.

He discovered a bot, an electronic program designed to forward information collected to an unknown source.

Intrigued someone could get past his firewalls and security,

Caleb investigated further. He considered who or what had the resources to hack into secure government facilities.

He traced the electronic trail, careful not to alert the perpetrator to his virtual presence. This person was good, one of the best he had seen in a long time.

This was interesting. The hacker's location was military centered. It wasn't one that he was familiar with. He tweaked it a bit more and smiled. He entered the unknown system.

Even though this was some secretive branch of the military, they had all the standard programs used by the official part of the organization. Caleb had worked on the security systems of military installations.

He smiled as he accessed the email account of his secret agent hacker.

His eyes opened in shock. Justin was his hacker?

"Wow!" though Caleb. "So this is the secret he's been hiding from him all these years." He noticed the word "Christian cell groups" in the subject line of one of the emails.

"Re: Report 131121:

"In regards to intel gathered on groups of Christians meeting in private homes to circumvent the ordinance against public gatherings. It has been decided that these meetings are deemed subversive by the government. Inform operatives to continue infiltration of said groups and set them up for forceable disbandment and re-education."

Caleb almost gave his presence away. He quickly refocused his attention and considered the possibilities. He would send out an alert to the cell leaders. They would have to take immediate actions to protect themselves.

He did another stealth search in Justin's computer and found the operatives infiltrating their ranks. He copied the file and would pass that along to the Elders to take care of.

Caleb placed his own data snoop program into Justin's computer. He wasn't sure the level of Justin's hacking abilities. It was still a surprise to him Justin had more than the standard everyday computer-user skills.

He knew his software was not detectable or traceable to the laptop he had specifically designated for this purpose. The information would be automatically forwarded through dozens of IP hops throughout the world.

Caleb left a command code in Justin's system, allowing him to access and take control of this computer and anything it was connected to. He backed out with his precious information, making sure his incursion and the spy he left behind would not be detected. When Caleb had successfully retreated, he put an alarm on the back door. The next time it was used, he would know when, by whom and what information they were attempting to obtain from the main data frame.

He leaned back in his chair and closed his eyes. The beginnings of an adrenaline headache was softly pounding in his head. He glanced over to the top right hand drawer and reached out to open it. He pulled out a bottle of Tylenol and swallowed a couple of pills. He then looked idly out of his window. From his position he could only see other sky scrapers and the sky.

"Oh, Lord," he prayed. "Your word declares that all things work for good to those who love You and are called according to Your purpose. I now understand the reason you allowed me to be shanghaied into this position, Father.

"I am honored You have chosen me to help protect Your flock from danger for a bit longer. Oh, Lord I look forward to the coming day when my faith will be rewarded by the sight of Your face and I can see the nail scars which bought my liberty."

Icthus

He wasn't sure how long he sat there in silent prayer, worshipping his General deep in the heart of enemy territory. He was the spy. He picked up the phone. "Carrie. Is there anything left on my calendar for today? No. Excellent! I'm going to make an early day of it today. You do the same. Have a good evening and see you tomorrow."

Icthus

Chapter Forty-seven

Justin slammed his hands on the table and glared at the men and women sitting around the table - a pile of reports spread out in front of him. Six infiltrations teams ready to pounce on their targets. Six failed missions in one day. This had not happened to him in his twenty plus years of service.

"Ok, you are telling me that the solid intel you have been gathering for months ended up being worthless? Each of you swear you were with the groups long enough to establish meeting patterns, how they contact each other, members' names and home addresses and now they seemed to have vanished into thin air?"

Administrative duties prevented Justin from going into the field anymore. However, he was in the control room monitoring the operation. He did not understand what happened when the teams moved on Church houses.

Teams were in place at the. People arrived at these homes in ones or twos over a couple of hours so as not to arouse suspicion. When team leaders were reasonably sure all targets were in place, the word was given and the trap was sprung.

They threw sonic grenades through the windows to stun the occupants inside. They rushed to the doors and smashed their way to capture their prey before they realized the net was empty. Well almost.

They did find their people unconscious and tied up in the bedrooms.

All six teams burst into empty houses. Puzzled, they swept them with infrared scanners, looking for body heat in hidden rooms in the houses and found nothing. Over seventy people had simply disappeared.

Further investigation in the basement of theses house churches revealed hidden tunnels leading out to underground mains where these people had exited several streets over, while the teams were waiting to enter the buildings.

Back up teams went to the individual homes of alleged leaders on the target list, only to find them vacant as well. Many looked like people where inside them. These Christians knew what was going to happen that night. Justin also knew it.

"Come on, people just don't vanish into thin air," Justin declared at the debriefing. "They must have gone somewhere."

Lieutenant Styles cleared his throat. "Sir, they didn't just disappear."

Justin looked at him. "It was rhetorical, Styles. I read the reports that there were tunnels leading to a nearby drain and they climbed out a couple of streets over. The question I have is how come our operatives did not know about this escape plan?"

They shifted uncomfortably in their seats as Justin pinned each one of them with a stare. The lieutenant spoke again. "Our infiltrators were unaware these tunnels existed. It is their opinion that only a select few knew about them, probably the leaders of the groups. We checked the other locations these groups were meeting in and found similar escape tunnels. Someone knew they would eventually be needed."

"What about the people who attended the meetings? Did we capture any of them at their places of work or their personal residences?"

Another uncomfortable silence ensued. Justin sneered. "You're telling me that each of these reports is accurate and that no one was apprehended from last night's raids?"

The newest member of this inner circle, Lieutenant Carslyle spoke up. "Well from what our infiltrators indicated, everyone only used their first names. Some of the addresses they gathered turned out to be empty lots or shopping malls. Employers of those targets where we knew they worked indicated they did not come in that morning."

Justin paced along the end of the table. "So, what we thought were individuals meeting in private homes to practice their illegal ceremonies turns out to be an organized network. Not only that, we have a spy in our ranks to warn them of upcoming actions planned against them."

The assembled group sat up straighter and shifted in their seats. A traitor in their midst was unthinkable. They began to protest, but Justin cut them off. "No, think about it. How did these people know they were going to be raided? They had to get their intel from someplace; someone."

"You seem to forget that we are fighting a war. It is no different than the work that we have been doing. Why are you surprised our own ranks have been somehow compromised?"

He turned and faced his team leaders once more. "Organization means there is a coordinated leadership involved. We need to hunt down that leadership." He pulled from his own memory. "Without a shepherd, the flock is scattered. We need to remove the flock's shepherds."

"Ok, we will meet here again at oh nine hundred and draw up a plan to snuff out this threat."

He watched them file out and then turned and walked through the connecting door to his office. So these sheep had a shepherd who knew the score. He sat down at his desk and leaned back in his chair and looked up at the ceiling. This assignment was taking an unexpected turn. He was not adverse to the unexpected. It offered a challenge.

He had to find the mole and plug the leak. He straightened up and pulled his keyboard to him. He started a security scan on his system and initiated a system wide one as well. Justin had not been a tech-head, as he used to call Caleb.

Being an active participant in the espionage game, he was an advocate of cyber security. It would take an exceptionally tech-savvy person to navigate through the firewalls and cyber traps built in to these ultra-secure systems.

After he initiated the scan he picked up his phone and dialed another number. "Can I speak to Caleb White, please? Tell him it's Justin and I need to meet with him as soon as possible."

Chapter Forty-eight

Caleb stared at his phone when Carrie informed him of Justin's request. He was positive Justin had not discovered the sniffer. Yet there was the possibility he had.

He breathed deeply in and slowly exhaled. "I must not jump to any conclusions," He said aloud.

In the short time the stealth had been planted, Caleb had amassed a great deal of knowledge of the counter terrorism unit.

After his discovery of the unit's directive he initiated the warning call to the leaders of the cell groups.

Before marshal law had been enacted Caleb had approached the leaderships of the Assembly with his concerns.

After much prayer and fasting, the Elders agreed with Caleb's assessment. They began preparations for the day when Christianity would be outlawed.

With the consensus of the members of the A   ssembly, they dissolved the official church organization and sold all of its assets.

They purchases several houses throughout the city and organized the cell groups. They would meet in these homes equipped with sophisticated monitoring systems and designed escape plans using the cities underground maze of storm drains.

They also created safe houses and locations where they could move a large number of people to safety quickly and then to a network of believers out of the city.

Caleb had been one of the architects of the system. With his connections in the tech industry he was able to access the best technology available. The chapel continued to function, meeting on a regular basis for Breaking of Bread, fellowship and spending time in God's Word and prayer.

The information he collected revealed Justin's organization had the names of the leaders of the six targeted cell groups in the organization and their members. All of their lives were in danger. He also had the names of the spies in their midst.

The plan had been activated. Cell members arrived for the Lord's Supper and Bible Study at their designated homes. They acted normally and disappeared inside. The infiltrators were quickly rendered unconscious and secured in one of the upstairs bedrooms.

The brethren went to the basements where most meetings were held. Normally the room would be set up with chairs circling small table holding a loaf of bread and a glass of wine in remembrance of the Lord's sacrifice.

Tonight it contained the small backpacks they had secreted into the house over the past two or three days. At one end of the room, which normally displayed a large wall-sized entertainment unit was a small doorway of which only the Elders had knowledge of. A sentry was in place with a laptop, monitoring the activities of the soldiers waiting to capture them.

They bent low and made their way through the tunnels to the storm drains coming out far enough not to alert the enemy. The Elders lead their members to an abandoned subway station.

Caleb had hacked the city's database and found this old station. He wiped all trace from the database. In a pinch it would hold a couple of hundred people. That night it served as refuge for seventy brothers and sisters.

Caleb met them and calmed their nerves. All the groups had

arrived safely. They thanked God and partook in the Lord's Supper. They had partitioned off the southern section of the station into temporary housing.

Cots lined up with bedding waiting to receive tired and frightened bodies. Rations and medical supplies were stored in steel cabinets. Banks of lockers were provided for the refugees.

At the one end of the station, was the command center. Caleb had installed a monitoring center. Together with some of his technical friends they had installed alarms and monitoring devices not only in the tunnel, but in the uncompromised safe houses and cells still active.

The Elders had watched the special ops teams invade the places where they thought they would find rich hauls of new fodder for the government re-education centers. They were pleased with the confused and angry reactions of the soldiers as their search of the houses came up empty.

Phase one of the plan had succeeded beyond their expectations. They bowed the knee to their Protector, giving thanks for His provisions.

Now Justin was on his to his office. Caleb thought it must be a coincidence. He found no evidence his friend discovered his complicity.

The buzzer on his intercom broke his reverie and he jumped slightly. He laughed at his overactive reaction imagination. "Yes, Carrie?"

"Major Jones is here to see you, Mr. White."

"Thank-you, Carrie, I will be right out."

He stood up and walked to the office door. He took a deep breath, and slowly opened the door. Justin was standing at Carrie's desk chatting with her. She was laughing at something he said. Justin straightened and smiled when he saw Caleb standing in the doorway. "Hey, buddy, how long has it been?"

Caleb walked over to him and they gave each other a hug. "I don't know. I guess about two years since you last crawled out from whatever rock you were hiding under at the time. I think we were in Dubai."

They laughed and Caleb escorted his friend into the office. "Carrie, can you hold all my calls?"

He didn't wait for her affirmative response and closed the door on the outer office. Justin was standing by the window overlooking the business district. "You know, Cal, we can almost see each other from our perspective offices."

Caleb laughed and smiled. "Now why would I want to look at your ugly mug?" He walked over to the bar. "Would you care for something to drink?" Caleb found it strategic to have a stocked bar in his office. It sometimes helped to relax his clients who were looking for solutions to their issues.

"Only water, please, I am on duty after all."

Caleb nodded and reached into the small refrigerator and pulled out two bottles. He walked over to the window and handed it to Justin. He opened the one still in his hand and took a drink. "So, how long have you been in the city? Last I heard you were in some Middle Eastern country doing whatever you do."

Justin laughed. "Been here a couple of months; keeping an eye on the military patrols. We don't want them to get too far out of hand with the people we were sworn to protect."

Caleb furrowed his brows. "If you can call it protecting."

Justin shook his head. "Look, Cal, I don't want to get into a morality debate here and now. I am looking for your IT services."

"Why? You should have access to some of the most up to date and sophisticated personnel in the world."

Justin looked at him. "Actually that is why I am coming to you. I have reason to believe that one of my people is acting outside the chain of command. I would like you to sweep my systems and see if you can locate any evidence of tampering."

Caleb leaned back in his chair in surprise. He was expecting to be arrested and become the latest guest of the government's re-education centers.

Justin continued. "I know you are a private consultant with the proper security clearance to work in government systems. I also know that you have been in this business a long time and have seen a lot of things the newer generation may not have come across."

He smiled. "A lot of our systems were also designed by your former employer. Who else would be so qualified? You are the best person for the job."

Caleb pulled out the keyboard tray and looked up his calendar. "What time frame are you looking at?"

They scheduled a time for him to come to the office and examine the systems.

Justin stood up and prepared to leave. "Thanks, Cal. I appreciate your taking the time to see me today and doing this for me. You are the only person I can trust to do this."

"You will think otherwise when you get the bill."

They laughed and Caleb escorted Justin to the elevators. He went back to his office and closed the door. He realized he was shaking.

Irony didn't exactly describe the situation: the spy being invited into the enemy lair to detect spyware he installed. He shook his head and chuckled. Who said God didn't have a sense of humor.

Chapter Forty-nine

Justin attempted to control his frustration. Seventy people disappeared from Greater Toronto Area. He knew that this was an orchestrated disappearance. He designed the disappearances of many people over the years and recognized the signs.

Caleb had gone over his systems with a virtual fine-toothed comb and gave the system a clean bill of health. Even his searches turned up nothing. If someone had hacked into this computer, they were very good: ghosts even. He could use technicians of this caliber. He was sure he had already recruited the best he could find.

He hated this feeling. Someone was watching his every move. He had a hunch and his hunches were rarely wrong. The Christians had a master mind calling the shots.

He went over the reports again: both the original ones and the more recent ones his operatives had submitted on this case. They chased down every rumor, any whisper of what had happened to these subversives. All the leads produced dead ends.

He realized all those people had gone to ground. He knew Christians were still active. He read the reports of people in parks and in restaurants talking about Jesus. It sounds like something Caleb would do. But all indications were his friend was no longer involved in Christian activities.

Justin had Caleb followed. The operative Indicated the man went to work, or traveled on work related business, attended the gym three or four times a week and went home. Justin stopped the surveillance after two weeks. He felt unease about investigating his old friend. He was relieved he could find no proof of Caleb's being complicit in these activities.

It had been two months since the aborted raids on the six targeted groups. During that time, all reported activity of these "house" churches had come back negative.

Other targeted houses under constant surveillance by both ground and satellite revealed no activity. They were abandoned as places of worships.

Justin examined the evidence he had amassed and recorded on several white boards now set up in his office. The houses had escape tunnels to the storm drains. They had discovered security and monitoring devices had been built into them and not obvious to people going in and out.

Justin swore at that last piece of information. The targets knew they were being watched and could see the teams as they waited to spring into action.

It turned out the houses belonged to non-existent people. Yet they were lived in, and cared for. The yards were neat, lawns mowed.

He had people examine city records, looking for clues for a staging area where so many people could have been sheltered and then smuggled out of the city undetected by military checkpoints.

They would need forged travel documents, photo identification and fake identities to successfully leave Toronto. It pointed to government level assistance to obtain the necessary paper work. He considered that last piece of information he wrote on the board. There were people on the inside providing this help.

He smiled. The trail just heated up again.

Chapter Fifty

Contrary to Justin's hypothesis Caleb was not in his apartment nor the gymn. He was sitting in a small coffee shop two blocks from work.

This was a hotspot for wireless and he often came here when it felt like the office walls were closing in on him. He had been working on the government contract over almost two years.

He maintained his offices in Toronto, able to do most of the work required remotely. Although officially working for the federal government, he was plugged into every level of government across the country.

During his tenure he had streamline databases, developed new software to protect it, found a hacker (Jason) and discovered what the government was really up to.

He smiled as he sipped his coffee. It was a techie's dream to control that much information of the powers that be. He was handed what many had attempted to gain illegally.

Unofficially, he used his position and security clearance to ensure the safety of many of the brothers and sisters. Those, like himself, were hunted by the government sworn to protect them. They were declared enemies of the state for claiming Jesus Christ as their Lord and Savior.

And he was one of them.

Caleb had worked with a couple of trusted brethren also working in the government. They set up the programing to create new identities for those in immediate danger of arrest. From any computer on the net, anyone in their network could create the necessary documents to leave the city legally.

From his consulting days, Caleb developed networks of

Christians all over the country. It seems the government concentrated their efforts in major cities and pretty much ignored rural areas. Caleb took advantage of this oversight while it was still viable.

The Elders refused to leave the city. They insisted that as long as there were believers trapped in the metropolis, it was their God-given duty to oversee their spiritual journey. There were still people who needed Christ and if all the Christians left, who would spread the Word?

Caleb realized sooner or later someone would put the pieces together and he would be sent for "re-education." He knew the term was an euphemism for execution for treason and crimes against humanity.

He understood it was important for the safety of his brothers and sisters, the fewer pieces of the network everyone knew the better. Most of them only knew three Assemblies, theirs, and the ones on either side of the network chain. A few, others like himself, maintained the flow of information and monitored cyber space for warnings of impending raids.

Caleb had come into contact with others like him in the major cities around the world. The news was much the same in other countries as well. Some places where Christianity had already been a crime, there was silence. He grieved for the churches there; he knew brethren in some of those places.

The work still went on. They baptized converts in makeshift containers when they couldn't safely do it in secluded park areas. People were being discipled and trained to carry the gospel message to those in this closing chapter of the Church Age.

Caleb had no doubt Christ's return was imminent. His personal study of Prophecy pointed to that. This was the Falling Away, mentioned by Paul to the Thessalonians. John in Revelation described this time in history in Christ's address to the church in Philadelphia:

"And to the angel of the church in Philadelphia write, 'These things says He who is holy, He who is true, "He who has the key of David, He who opens and no one shuts, and shuts and no one opens": "I know your works. See, I have set before you an open door, and no one can shut it; for you have a little strength, have kept My word, and have not denied My name.

"Indeed I will make those of the synagogue of Satan, who say they are Jews and are not, but lie—indeed I will make them come and worship before your feet, and to know that I have loved you. Because you have kept My command to persevere, I also will keep you from the hour of trial which shall come upon the whole world, to test those who dwell on the earth.

"Behold, I am coming quickly! Hold fast what you have, that no one may take your crown. He who overcomes, I will make him a pillar in the temple of My God, and he shall go out no more. I will write on him the name of My God and the name of the city of My God, the New Jerusalem, which comes down out of heaven from My God. And I will write on him My new name."

He thought of the Chinese proverb, "May you live in interesting times." He was certainly in those times. Instead of despair, there was hope, instead of death there was life, instead of doom there was release.

People fell into two camps; the ones who rejected Jesus Christ and God's offer of salvation and those who were seeking for more than this life could offer. As long as God allowed, Caleb would fight the good fight on earth to make sure the gospel was presented.

He stood up from the table and headed toward the door. Before going back outside he did up his overcoat and put on his gloves. It was late December and the wind was picking up.

He missed the Christmas programs that abounded this time of year. It had been one of those rare times when much of the world stopped to pay homage to a God whom they regularly spat in his face.

He walked the street back to his office he noticed the brightly lit shops. There were Santa's and elves in every window. However,the staple red pots of the Salvation Army were missing: there were no carolers on the streets.

In spite of appearances, it was not a joyful time anymore. Well, joyful for those who had money to spend on the unending parties which were still very much a part of the season.

Caleb kept in touch with his parents. He had not had the opportunity to go to his house on Sand Bay last summer as he had in the past. Caleb had warned them about the trouble in Toronto.

They had an idea the same was occurring there in the smaller cities as well. Because they were in a rural area, they were left alone for the most part. They also knew that would only be temporary.

His parents took his warnings concerning the mass arrests in churches in the big cities and took steps to circumvent it from happening in their small country church. The Assembly members held an emergency meeting.

They officially dissolved the ministry and started to meet in each other's homes. They were a small group of people, but this prevented them from being arrested wholesale and shipped off to the re-education centers.

The Elders overseeing the Goulais River assembly also agreed to assist Caleb to be a stop in the network to move hunted Christians from one location to another.

The assembly had already hidden and passed on several people since the crackdown on the house churches in Toronto. Caleb was correct in his assessment rural areas of the country would not be a high priority for the counter terrorism units. They had concentrated on the major urban centers.

This allowed for rural believers to prepare themselves for the persecutions which would be arriving all too soon. They knew that when the cities were under control, then the government would turn to them.

They didn't have the luxury of the underground systems in the large cities, so they took advantage of the caves in the nearby hills. They were stockpiled with supplies for several months as well as a communications center set up to work off of the wireless towers in the area.

Each member of the Assembly was assigned to go to one of the caves if they came under attack. To keep everyone as safe as possible, members were only given two locations: one as the primary destination and a secondary if they could not reach the first one.

Mr. White and Mr. Collins were now Elders at North Woods. They were the only two who knew the location of their entire network. As a part of the larger Christian underground movement, they were only aware of the next two closest Assemblies.

Like their counterparts in the larger cities, they were committed to protecting their charges and training them not only in the Word, but how to survive In this new World order.

Caleb shook himself out of his reverie. He walked through the doors of the office tower where his office was located. He entered the elevator and rode it up to the penthouse floor.

He looked at his fellow passengers. He always thought strange that people got on an elevator and all of them stared at the floor numbers as they flashed by. They rarely talked to each other. They just kept staring at the numbers as they flashed on and off. The people got on and off. He knew many of them by site; most of them worked in the same building.

He stepped off the elevator on his floor, and walked towards his office. He smiled at Carrie as he walked past her desk and turned the handle on his own space there.

He sat down at his desk, but instead of pulling up his system he stared out of the window. Caleb had a feeling that his time was short here. He felt his job was almost done and he needed to be thinking of his next move: a move that would take him off the grid.

Chapter Fifty-one

In early February when Caleb discovered the planned re-education of the rest of the country was scheduled to roll out that spring. He still had the sniffer planted in Justin's computer. Justin had not suspected it was there. He left the back door his friend had created. Once he discovered the type of information Justin was searching for, he carefully rewrote the program. It reported misleading information.

He often thought of the strangeness of his position. The Bible taught submission to the government, but here he was breaking the law. By definition he was an enemy of state. Justin and his Black Ops teams had the legal blessings of this government to hunt him and others like him.

As he harvested more data from Justin's computer, he learned the detention centers where concentration camps. People who opposed the government and the policies it was enacting were gathered there for re-education. Drug therapy and brain washing were the desired methods of treatment. People who refuse to conform to the regime disappeared.

People lived in terror. Families had been torn apart as children were set against parents. Fathers turned in sons, daughters reported their mothers for "subversive" activities.

He contacted his father through a secure channel and told them of the upcoming cleansing operations. Caleb was not able to provide an accurate date, other than by the end of April. Mr. White, in turn, activated the chain in his area, informing his contacts in the other Assemblies. Within a few hours, the entire Assembly network of Northern Ontario would be aware the persecutors were coming.

Mr. White cleared his cell phone of all the contacts it contained.

To their neighbors, they appeared as the typical retired couple. That was what they were supposed to think. They started destroying any papers and other materials which could tie them into other members in their local Assembly or in their part of the network.

They quietly moved their own personal supplies to the cave where they would take refuge from the army sweeps. Other members of the assembly were also taking similar precautions. They would be ready for the coming persecutions.

Chapter Fifty-two

Justin was not totally surprised when he found that he would be assuming operations in Northern Ontario. Toronto was pretty much under control. He was from the area and had still had a lot of contacts there: albeit old ones.

He was still stumped to the mole that had invaded his own offices. He did not make that information known to his superiors. What they expected of him were results. He got the job done and the only one who cared how it got done was Major Justin Jones.

He asked if sending him to his former home wouldn't be considered a conflict of interest. They felt that after the time away from the area, the answer should be no. They concluded he should have a distinct edge rounding up subversives their due to the contacts he had in the area.

So the last part of March was spent briefing his replacement in Toronto on where the mission objectives stood in relation to being completed. Justin was proud to inform the new commander that they were on target with mission objectives and achieving their targets. He glossed over the failure to round up Christians after the first major push.

It appeared to him most of them bugged out of the city. He knew that they were out there, but they were not behaving as people who were taken totally by surprise. When they managed to arrest the occasional one in the streets, they had little to offer in terms of where the cell groups were located other than their own circle.

He could not determine where their spy was as well. This ghost in their system had successfully derailed this part of the plan and only this part. Their timetable had not been seriously compromised, but Justin found it irritating just the same.

What made it more difficult was he was not fighting terrorists with weapons aimed directly at him. He was at war on a level he had not experience before. He was fighting his own country men and their beliefs which they had held as a matter of right since Canada had been founded.

Justin was apprehensive about moving home and setting up operations. This time it would not be just names on a report that he would be dealing with. This time it would be faces he knew attached to those names. Faces and names of people he would be sending to their deaths.

Chapter Fifty-three

It was three weeks before the traditional celebration of Easter when Caleb felt the Holy Spirit indicate it was time for him to leave the city.

He had been planning to this end since the New Year started. Due to his security clearance and the nature of his work he had not been allowed to leave Toronto, unless it was to travel to Ottawa or another major center to work on the Government databases.

He often suspected his activities had been detected. No one came to arrest him and escort him off to the nearest detention center. He kept his guard up and paid careful attention to everything he did in order to keep his covert activities secret as long as could.

He set up fake credentials for himself as he had done for so many of his brothers and sisters. He was truly grateful for God's guidance and mercy. He had broken so many laws that he would be summarily executed if he was discovered.

As he prepared his departure, he wondered if he was doing this to avoid being captured. He knew that should the Lord delay His return he would be caught eventually.

He wasn't sure if it mattered if it was here or somewhere else. He would be doing something similar elsewhere. He was sworn to serve one Lord and go whereever he was directed to.

He warned the brothers and sisters working with him on his feelings. They were in agreement. It was time to go.

It was not Caleb White who boarded a plane that early April morning headed for Sault Ste. Marie and home. It was Joe Smith on business. He breathed a sigh of relief as he settled into his seat on the small jet. He expected at any moment to have sirens go off and guards dragg him off the plane and into a waiting black van.

The flight was uneventful. He was able to view Lake Superior from his vantage point. It was so huge it rarely froze completely over. Usually he could take a drive up Highway Seventeen to Alona Bay Lookout and see the ice floating on the water being driven by waves onto the shore. Further along. Mystery Bay and Old Woman Bay you could find ice caves created by the actions of the wind and waves.

As teenagers he, Justin and some of their buddies would go there during the winter to climb ice cliffs which formed from the stormy waves of an angry Lake Superior. He gave himself a shake of his head. It was and activity their parents were never made aware of.

Winter time was also for skiing at Searchmont or Buttermilk, cross country at Stokely Creek or snowmobiling beside the Algoma Central Railway tracks.

He got off the plane and experienced the same trepidation as he picked up his luggage and went to the car rental kiosk to pick up the Jeep Wrangler he was driving under his assumed name. He felt it would be better this way instead of having someone pick him up and be recognized and arrested.

He left the airport and drove towards home for the last time. He turned up Peoples' Road and took the short cut out of town to the Fifth line and headed north. He would return the vehicle tomorrow. Someone would follow him to pick him up. He had his own truck parked at his home on Sand Bay.

He wondered if the shallow bay was still covered with a sheet of ice this time of year. He knew it was probably too late to do a little ice fishing.

Chapter Fifty-four

Justin's new office in the Station Towers overlooked the Sainte Mary's River. From there he looked out on the International Bridge connecting his Sault Ste. Marie with its American counterpart. He could see Lake Superior State University across the water. To the left was the Tower of History, a landmark in the Michigan city.

To the right of the bridge he could make out the steel plant: a staple industry for over a century. In front of the steel plant, to the right of the local power generating station was another staple from another era: the paper mill. It ceased operations years ago. The sandstone facade of the building had been taken from the excavations for the locks near the end of the nineteenth century.

An enterprising entrepreneur had turned the old papermill site into a triving event destination for everything from weddings to outdoor concerts. It had done quite well: until such gatherings were declared illegal.

He thought it rather ironic that the most secretive arm of the military and of the government was now afforded space in office buildings instead of secret bunkers buried in the ground.

Those bunkers existed, but such a base did not exist here. There wasn't even a regular forces base, only the Pine Street Armory which headquartered the Twenty-sixth and Forty-ninth Reserve regiments.

His home and the smaller urban areas were considered secondary targets after they subdued the major centers. This mostly conservative city of seventy-five thousand and other similar sized cities had survived the chaos which reigned in the larger ones. The police force and reservists were more than adequate for keeping order.

The shortages were here as well as in the larger cities, but saner heads prevailed during the worst of the riots. The local militia and the police forces were able to maintain control.

He was here to oversee the implementation of the government's objectives: to hunt out and eradicate subversive groups which by now had escaped from the first round of detentions in the larger cities.

He felt a little uneasy being here. In Toronto and Ottawa there was little chance of running into old party buddies. He wondered how he would feel if he was the one to neutralize Mr. or Mrs White. Could he honestly coral Jo's parents and watch as the black vans took them to the detention centers?

He had been here a week. He had his own personal team with him. Because this was a smaller operation, he would probably be partaking in some of the raids. He also met with the local militia commanders and set out to create a coordinated plan.

He wasn't sure how these volunteers would react when they were required to actively pursue subversive groups. This was vastly different than ensuring curfews were met and unauthorized public gatherings broken up. They probably had the same misgivings as he did.

He turned from the view and sat down at his desk. He opened his laptop and waited for it to come out of sleep. He glanced at the digital clock on the wall. It was almost time for the video conference.

He logged into the conference and watched as the participants appeared on the small windows on his desktop. They were his counterparts in other offices across the country. All of them were committed to the same goals.

Of all the groups they hunted, there was one that was becoming a thorn in their sides. It had been fairly straight forward to disband the anarchist elements. The homeless were a matter of doing a street round up. Other anti-government factions had been poorly organized and were easy prey for them.

The only group that seemed to flourish the more they were hunted was the Church. Justin had thought Christianity was gone when he was a teenager. He was finding out thirty years later that wasn't the case.

He kept tabs on his acquaintances from his past life. They had appeared for all intents and purposes have given up on their religious activities. He was surprised when he discovered shortly after the government declared martial law, North Woods Chapel ceased operations.

General Smith, his first commanding officer and now the person in charge of the counter terrorism unit, was calling the meeting to order. "Congratulations on your promotion, Colonel Jones."

"Thank-you General Smith. Same to you."

"Have you settled into your new digs yet?"

"Yes, sir. I was thinking how normal we've become, sitting in office buildings instead of out of sight."

"Well we are still out of sight, figuratively, Colonel. As far as the country is concern, we are liaison and recruiting offices."

The General cleared his throat. "We need to address this problem with the Christians. They are better organized than the Mafia was."

Justin was watching his pointer move through a visual presentation which accompanied the General's report. It had been gathered through the various intelligence operatives funneling through their offices up the chain of command.

"Our objective with this mission is to eliminate the threat these people pose to our government's agenda to create a united society."

Justin was absently nodding as the General outlined the plan of attack. "Coming up is the most important date to the Christians. It is the observation of what used to be Easter. We think that they will be lulled into a false sense of security and be easier to round up."

"Colonel Jones." Justin snapped his head up and stared at the screen. "Here is something that I think will be of interest to you. Our latest intel indicates the master mind of the Toronto disappearances has left for northern pastures."

Justin raised his eyebrows. "Well that is interesting. Any information on his destination?"

The General nodded. "I am sending you the updated intel now."

"Copy that, General."

"Ok ladies and gentlemen, is everyone clear on our objectives and timetables?"

There was affirmative assent from the parties involved in the conference. The General closed the meeting and the video feeds started to flick off.

Justin waited and pulled up the file General Smith had sent him. He smiled as he viewed the intel. He believed revenge was a dish best served cold. He was looking forward to finding his nemesis. And eliminating him or her.

Chapter Fifty-five

It was Sunday Evening. Traditionally much of the Christian world observed this day as Palm Sunday: the day the Lord rode a donkey into Jerusalem presenting Himself as the Messiah. Caleb was meeting with his brothers and sisters in one of the caves set up as a refuge in King Mountain.

He thought it appropriate that they were worshipping their King in this place. There were about a dozen people gathered to honor and remember Jesus Christ in the manner of the early church.

They were seated in a circle around a table with a loaf of bread and a cup of wine. The participants sat quietly around these elements. Some were silently praying, others leafing through their Bibles.

Caleb's old friend Duncan stood up to speak. "I felt the Lord speaking to me regarding the passage in first Thessalonians four, verses thirteen to eighteen, *'But I do not want you to be ignorant, brethren, concerning those who have fallen asleep, lest you sorrow as others who have no hope.'For if we believe that Jesus died and rose again, even so God will bring with Him those who sleep in Jesus.*

'For this we say to you by the word of the Lord, that we who are alive and remain until the coming of the Lord will by no means precede those who are asleep. For the Lord Himself will descend from heaven with a shout, with the voice of an archangel, and with the trumpet of God. And the dead in Christ will rise first.

'Then we who are alive and remain shall be caught up together with them in the clouds to meet the Lord in the air. And thus we shall always be with the Lord. Therefore comfort one another with these words.'

He gave a sad smile. "It is not a secret that the time of the Church is coming to an end." He gestured at their rocky surroundings. "We are hunted for our belief in the Lord Jesus Christ. But all is not bleak and dark. Our future is one of promise. We will be with the Lord. I don't know about you, but I am listening every day for that shout and blast of trumpet."

People around him chuckled. "I take comfort in this passage: *'we which are alive and remain shall be caught up together with them in the clouds to meet the Lord in the air.'*"

"We call this service a remembrance of His sacrifice on Calvary. I would like to remind us when we break bread we are also looking forward to the time when we will partake of these elements with Christ in glory. We have hope; those who persecute us do not have the hope of glory."

People nodded as Duncan sat back down. Caleb smiled. This time was always special to him. Brothers and sisters worshipping the Lord and sharing what He has laid upon the hearts of individual lives.

He looked around the circle of believers. His parents were with him today as well as his former in-laws. There were a few other familiar faces as well as a mix of new ones. He smiled. Christ was adding daily to His Church all those who would be saved.

Even in these dark hours, there was a beacon of light shining for the souls of men.

Caleb stood up and opened his Bible. He thumbed through the worn pages and stopped at Hebrews 12. "Friends, I too feel the time is short. We are in the home stretch where endurance counts for much to get us to the finish line. It is not speed at this point, but finding the inner strength Christ provides for us to push through to the end." He looked down at the book in his hands.

'Therefore we also, since we are surrounded by so great a cloud of witnesses, let us lay aside every weight, and the sin which so easily ensnares us, and let us run with endurance the race that is set before us, looking unto Jesus, the author and finisher of our faith, who for the joy that was set before Him endured the cross, despising the shame, and has sat down at the right hand of the throne of God.'

"I particularly like this passage. It refers to Jesus as the author and finisher of our faith. Like a writer who creates his characters and has developed the story for them to finish. We follow them as they work to overcome the challenges and how they change or grow to the end of the story.

"Jesus has written our lives out. He loves us and is standing at the line marked 'the end.' But it is only the end of one stage of our lives. He endured the journey that was His on this earth. He finished that course and sat down at the right hand of God. He sits there waiting until the day of Wrath, the coming tribulation.

"Our journey doesn't take that road. We will not face this time, but we will partake in the marriage supper of the Lamb described in Revelation. All tears will be forever past, all the pain gone in the overcoming joy of being in the presence of our Lord and Savior."

He bowed his head. "Great and gracious Lord, we come to you in eager anticipation of Your coming. Help us to withstand the testing and persecution which has started as the world system strives to expunge you from man's memory. You will prevail and we have hope in this world that only you can provide.

"We thank you for the bread on this table which symbolizes your body which was sacrificed for our sins. We pray this in your Son's precious and holy name, Amen."

Caleb stood and approached the table in the center of the circle. He picked up the loaf of bread symbolizing Christ's body and broke it into three parts. He picked up the tray it was on and walked back to the circle where he handed it to the person sitting beside him.

The person broke off a small piece and put it in his mouth and passed the tray to the next person. The tray made its way around the circle until it came back to where Caleb was sitting. He took the plate and also broke off a piece of bread. After a few minutes he stood up and returned the bread to the table.

They sat in quiet contemplation for a few minutes. Mr. Collins stood and prayed. "Father we thank you for the promise you made to Adam and Eve in the Garden of Eden, that you would send us a Redeemer. We remember the blood of the Holy One spilt to buy us back from the bondage of sin. As we partake of the cup, we are reminded of the New Covenant you with your chosen people Israel and to which you have already made us members. We look forward to the day when we will partake of the cup together with you in your kingdom. Amen"

Like Caleb, Mr. Collins walked over to the table and picked up the cup of wine now sitting beside the broken loaf. He walked back to the circle and handed it to Caleb and sat down. Caleb took a sip and passed it on to the next person.

When the last person had taken a sip of wine, Mr. Collins returned the cup and sat down again. They sang a closing song and stood up and started to rearrange the chairs for the next meeting. Someone gathered up the song books and returned them to their place on a nearby shelf. Another person picked up the plate and cup and put them away. The table was also moved out of the way.

They were being hunted to extinction, but here they were, as their brothers and sisters had gathered over two thousand years before. They had come together for worship, encouragement, and to spend time in God's Word.

Back at his home on the shores of Lake Superior, Caleb looked out over the partially thawed bay. Near to the shore, the ice sheet gave the appearance of solidity, but the warmer spring weather was already working to rot away the vestiges of winter.

Beyond the bay area, he could see the moonlight reflect off the open water. The warmer weather had melted most of the snow and when he drove past the river he noticed the ice was turning a dirty brown as the river underneath was fighting to break free from its icy prison.

He turned from the window and walked over to the airtight woodstove which heated the house. He opened the door and loaded it with a fresh supply of year old maple. With the drafts closed, the fire would burn all night.

He sat down in his favorite recliner chair and resumed staring out of the window. His thoughts were still on the meeting he attended a few hours ago. He had a feeling these special moments were numbered.

He wanted to take advantage of the apparent lull in the hostile and forcible removal of Christians from society before the secret police moved in for what they would consider the final kill.

He knew that this persecution was only the beginning. When the true church was removed, during the tribulation period, a person calling on the name of Christ for salvation would pay for it with his life.

Whether it was the Holy Spirit's prompting or his own fond memories, he was thinking of celebrating the resurrection of Jesus Christ on The Bluffs. He would praise and worship Him as the sun rose that Easter morning.

He prayed that Justin was still in Toronto. He often wondered how his old friend would have reacted if he ever discovered he was the object of their manhunt, the perceived leader of the Christians.

Caleb had never really considered himself a leader of the Assembly. He was a teacher and God had placed him in a position where his talents were best suited. His monitoring of Justin's computer system had alerted him to the fact they had realized the exodus of Christians from the urban areas had largely been the work of one person who had access to government systems.

He knew that his largely undetected actions were nothing short of a miracle of grace from God's hands. He marveled at constantly seeing God at work in his life: his faith rewarded over and over.

He stood up and turned out the lights. He would rely on God's grace one more time on the top of The Bluffs where he would honor his Lord at the rising of the sun.

Chapter Fifty-six

Justin finished his final briefing with the team leaders for the offensive they would conduct two days from now. This was Friday, but not a normal Friday. This was the Friday when Christians observed the memory of the crucifixion of Jesus Christ.

During his teen years he would often attend services at North Woods, less often as he neared adulthood and turned his back on Christianity. He kept up that charade for a few years after he left and joined the army, but he realized that he had not fooled everybody.

Justin knew Caleb put the pieces of the puzzle together by the time they graduated from high school. His friend had asked pertinent questions to Justin and several times brought the discussion back to spiritual issues in an attempt to force Justin to reconsider the road he was starting to travel.

One of the last nights such a discussion took place was during a camp out on The Bluffs. They were laying under the early summer sky a couple of weeks before graduation. Caleb banked the small campfire for the night and they had crawled into their sleeping bags. "I always think of Psalm nineteen on nights like this." said Caleb.

"Come on, Cal, it's not Sunday morning yet."

"I'm not about to preach a sermon. But I wonder if David was looking at a night sky similar to this when he had the inspiration to pen those words: *'The heavens declare the glory of God; And the firmament shows His handiwork. Day unto day utters speech and night unto night reveal knowledge. There is no speech nor language where their voice is not heard. Their line has gone out through all the earth and their words to the end of the world.'"*

Caleb continued, "David was writing about the light waves that come from the stars thousands of years before man even knew what they were. Every time we see a star or even stand in the light of our own sun, we are seeing them praise their Creator."

"Justin, when was the last time you praised your Creator?"

He sat up and glared at Caleb. "You may want to preach all night, but I want to go fishing at first light. Now be quiet so I can get some sleep."

Caleb backed down that time and never pushed the issue after that point.

Justin shook his head to clear the attack of nostalgia. He had more pressing matters at hand. In two days they would crush the rebellion in this area.

His intel had confirmed the leader of the group in Toronto was indeed in this area and he was looking forward to finding this person and personally ending his life.

He was thankful Caleb was still in Toronto. He came to the conclusion his friendship would be over when he found out who was in charge of arresting his parents.

He and his team members planned their strategy. Based on the information they gleaned from their sources, they set the traps carefully to capture their prey. He thought about all of the places where these Christians were most likely to meet to observe Easter morning. He realized there was one place guaranteed to produce results: The Bluffs. He would lead that team personally.

Chapter Fifty-seven

Caleb took the lead hiking up the trail to the top of The Bluffs in the predawn darkness of Resurrection morning. He was not surprised when several of the brothers and sisters expressed the same desire to commemorate this special day the same way he was.

The feeling of nostalgia had little to do with their decision. They felt the same Caleb did. This was no ordinary day and the Holy Spirit was leading them to this place.

They decided to draw as little attention to themselves as possible. They would arrive at the start of the hiking trail mostly in ones and twos and start up the mountain at five minute intervals.

Caleb started up the trail first. Every few yard he broke a glow stick and dropped it on the ground to show the way for those following. He realized that the trail would not be the easiest to follow, but it would draw less attention than people using flashlights.

In addition to the glow sticks, Caleb carried a canteen of wine and a package of mozza, the traditional flat Jewish bread eaten at Passover. It would survive a hike in better condition than a loaf of bread.

He reached the summit of the cliff and looked out over the dark valley. The top was pretty much as he had remembered it. The moon had set and a blanket of stars visible in the pre-dawn darkness.

The others were arriving. He quickly started a small fire in the fire pit. It was a risk doing this, but they had come too far to stop now.

The last of the hikers arrived and it was time to begin. They were quietly talking to each other as they gathered around the fire. They subsided into silence as they started to pray and worship their Savior.

Someone started to sing How Great Thou Art. The rest of the group joined in. The strains of the song died away and someone prayed. Caleb didn't know everyone who had made the trek here this morning. What he knew was God was in this place with them.

One after another, people shared a testimony, a song, a favorite Scripture passage. The sky overhead had started to lighten when they gave thanks for the elements and passed them from hand to hand.

They had just finished partaking of the wine when the attack came. The bushes came alive with soldiers bearing guns. Some one screamed and chaos broke out as people panicked and attempted to flee, only to be brought down by tazers, their bodies jerking as the electrical currents disrupted the ability to move their muscles.

Some people were forced to the ground with the butt ends of rifles, their heads bleeding from the wounds. Caleb could hear people crying and praying for help. Others were rejoicing, knowing that they were considered worthy to suffer for their Lord's sake.

He stood quietly by the dying fire. One of the soldiers moved toward him, pistol raised in his hand. He bowed his head and commended his soul to his creator and looked up again into the shocked eyes of his old friend.

"Caleb!"

Chapter Fifty-eight

Justin stared in shock at Caleb as the rays of the rising sun started to appear over the ridge on the other side of the valley. His team corralled the uninjured detainees. They were waiting his command to escort them to the vans at the base of the bluff that would take them to the detention center.

"Why did it have to be you?" he asked.

Caleb smiled. "I have my mission as well, Justin, Old friend."

"No... You are not supposed to be here. I checked. You are supposed to be in Toronto. What are you doing here?"

"I'm worshipping Christ, Justin. You ought to know that."

Justin was aware the rest of his team was watching the exchange. They knew their standing orders were to neutralize the leadership of subversive groups.

They looked at each other and wondered why their commanding officer was not carrying out an objective of their mission.

Justin realized they were staring at him: captors and captives. "Take the prisoners to the vans." He turned back to Caleb.

"I came home for Easter, Justin. I haven't been up here in years. My parent's are not able to make this climb anymore. I led them up here to watch the sunrise in honor of the Son who rose from the dead."

Justin shook his head. "NO! I don't believe that any more. Christianity was outlawed along with all other beliefs not sanctioned by the state. What are you doing?"

"It isn't the first time a government has attempted to wipe out Christians as enemies of the state. It won't be the last."

"Justin, even now, the door is still open for you. You know the way to Jesus."

He shook his head. "I have truly sold my soul. I have sworn to uphold the law. That includes removing perceived threats to the country: Islam, Christianity, Judaism. All of it declared not to be compatible with the agenda of the government."

Justin went on. "I killed people to protect our country. I spied and toppled regimes in order to protect you."

Bitterly he spat on the ground. "You were too freaking stubborn to deny your faith and support the government."

Caleb smiled gently at Justin. "Our government has become fascist and is no better than the Nazis of World War Two or the communist regimes of Russia and China. I have known the score for quite some time. The Bible predicted the world would I come to this. I have never stopped believing it."

"Justin. It doesn't matter what the government has done. God runs the show. You have to carry out your duties. You have no control over me unless He grants it."

"I'm truly surprised." said Justin. "I thought that you would have turned your back for good on God when Jo died. But instead it has made you stronger."

"If you know so much about me, you should know that I almost turned away from it. Instead I grew closer to God.

"It took several years to reach that point. For a very long time I was angry with God for taking my wife. I had to work through the grief before I was ready to resume my relationship with Him. It was only when I reached that point I realized He was in control and had worked to bring me back to His arms. Jo's death was devastating to me, but God made it for good, as He promised."

"I was free to travel and spread the gospel where ever and when ever. I saw how Christians lived in other parts of the world; the good and the bad. I desperately wish the Jo could have been with me. I am looking forward to seeing her very soon.

"God put me in a position to bring glory to Him and I was a willing soldier.

"You know what you have to do, Justin."

Justin shook his head. "I can't! You are my only true friend."

Caleb shook his head. "No Justin, you have another true friend; the same one who called us so many years ago. He is still here, waiting for you with open arms, Justin. You can still accept His offer of salvation. It doesn't matter what you have done in the past. All is forgiven."

Justin looked at the detainees now being herded down the mountain. He recognized a few of the people who had been arrested. He grew up with them; used to go to church with them. He turned and looked at his friend one last time. "Caleb..."

There were tears in his eyes as he pointed his revolver at Caleb. His hand was shaking. He knew his orders. His finger slowly contracted the trigger. "My brother..."

Caleb looked up. He gave a smile. "Do you hear trumpets?"

And Caleb had vanished before his eyes. He quickly scanned the area to see that the detainees had also disappeared. His team was staring at him, confused. They had just witnessed the strangest escape they have every encountered: their prisoners disappeared in thin air.

A blinding flash of light caught his attention. In the direction of the city several mushroom clouds rose above it. The last thing on earth Justin saw was the giant mushroom cloud in the distance as the blast wave hit him.

"And in Hell He lifted up his eyes..."

THE END

People have asked for it

You've met Caleb, God's choice for masterminding the escape network and working to keep Christians safe from the government which had declared their beliefs illegal and made them pay for not paying homage to the Agenda.

Now meet the man who Engineered their escape into the wilderness of Northern Ontario.

Coming Soon by **Bible School Dropout Publications**

Focal Point

Book Two in the Icthus Series

Icthus

Dave used the night vision goggles to survey the train yards. There were no guards visible, which is what their intelligence had indicated. All security was controlled from an office which monitored the perimeter with cameras. The person who sat in the office, sipping stale coffee and observing the feed from the perimeters cameras had no idea he was watching looped images of the yard he was protecting.

Dave felt more than a little uneasy the National Security Forces would leave such a strategic location for the successful movement of goods and services with only camera monitoring, which they had demonstrated could be manipulated fairly easily.

The three men who had volunteered for this mission would have a total of fifteen minutes to installed their monitoring equipment on the trains. They would broadcast similar information the National Security Forces cameras except would provide feedback to their intelligence the impression the trains were running from Sault Ste. Marie to Hearst the way they were supposed to and not record anything out of the ordinary.

Dave consulted his watch and nodded to the other men. They tossed out a couple of thumbs up.

Karl cut the fence with a laser torch and accessed the yard. They crossed the tracks to the locomotive which would leave in Just a few hours to make its northern run.

Dave looked over at Jake, gave him the thumbs up and stepped on the steps to climb onto the engine. The man returned the gesture and turned and repeated the gesture to Karl who clambered on board the front of the locomotive to the newly mounted cameras.

Dave had been surprised by the amount of information Caleb was able to provide on the locomotives and the video feeds the National Security Force had installed and they were able to get the counter feeds together quickly.

They worked quickly, installing their own equipment on the locomotive. They were careful enough to conceal the devices. At first glance, the equipment would look like normal military intelligence units. Unless the National Security Forces came with their specialists and swept for the new devices, they would be undetectable. There was no need for people to be on the machine: unless the engine or cars developed major mechanical issues.

David glanced at his watch and spotted Jake and Karl who gave him thumbs up. He nodded.

It was time to go.

They quickly jumped off the train and started across the rails back to their escape point.

Lights came on, startling the men. From several of the cars and the surrounding buildings a dozen National Security Force soldiers quickly surrounded them. One of them came forward and examined their faces intently. He stopped and stared at Dave. A small smile played at the corner of his lips.

"Well, Mr. Saunderson. You are a long way from Rio." Said Justin.

Hi, I'm the author *of The Bible School Dropout's Bigger and Better Guide to Bible Study, The Bible School Dropout's Guide to More Bible Study, Xtreme Xianity, Core Elements, In Hot Pursuit* and The Name of the Lord is series. I am also the author of the novels *Free* and *Icthus.*

These Bible studies are based upon inductive Bible study methods which use grammatical-historical, normal or literal methods of interpretation. If you can ask the questions; who, what, where, why, when and how, then you can do an inductive Bible study.

I really am a Bible school dropout. I left Bible school at the beginning of my third year. But that was not the end of my Christian experience and I have been actively teaching and writing study material for over 30 years.

It doesn't matter if you have had formal training or not. Anyone with the right tools and practice can study their Bible for themselves. I encourage people to learn what it has to say instead of letting others tell them what it says.

If you enjoyed this book, please go to the Amazon website and leave a book review.

Feedback and suggestions are welcome. Drop a line to bibleschooldropout@gmail.com. You can also visit my website www.bibleschooldropout.com.

Icthus

www.ingramcontent.com/pod-product-compliance
Lightning Source LLC
Chambersburg PA
CBHW070330260626
47160CB00003B/1002